"I'm bee

Jonathon was quiet for a moment and finally tapped Leah on the shoulder until she turned to face him.

"I wouldn't mind being your lover, either—not a bit," he said distinctly. "I don't expect it will happen tonight . . . or next week . . . or any special time soon. But I think it will happen. There are certain feelings between us. You know what I mean."

Right to the point and dead on target. She couldn't believe anyone could be blunt and honest and yet guileless. He'd made a statement, not thrown her a line to test the waters.

"I guess I do. The question I've been asking myself is whether to give those feelings any expression. They've brought me trouble in the past."

"It's not the feelings that bring trouble," he whispered. "It's who they're attached to. I'm not trouble, Leah."

She tended to agree, and was about to, when Jonathon Jericho Wardwell gave her the longest, most thorough and best kiss Leah had gotten in ages.

Dear Reader,

Welcome to Silhouette! Our goal is to give you hours of unbeatable reading pleasure, and we hope you'll enjoy each month's six new Silhouette Desires. These sensual, provocative love stories are both believable and compelling—sometimes they're poignant, sometimes humorous, but always enjoyable.

Indulge yourself. Experience all the passion and excitement of falling in love along with our heroine as she meets the irresistible man of her dreams and together they overcome all obstacles in the path to a happy ending.

If this is your first Desire, I hope it'll be the first of many. If you're already a Silhouette Desire reader, thanks for your support! Look for some of your favorite authors in the coming months: Stephanie James, Diana Palmer, Dixie Browning, Ann Major and Doreen Owens Malek, to name just a few.

Happy reading!

Isabel Swift
Senior Editor

SDRL-7/85

ANN HURLEY
A Fair Breeze

Silhouette Desire

Published by Silhouette Books New York
America's Publisher of Contemporary Romance

SILHOUETTE BOOKS
300 East 42nd St., New York, N.Y. 10017

Copyright © 1986 by Ann Hurley

ISBN: 0-373-05321-5

First Silhouette Books printing December 1986

America's Publisher of Contemporary Romance

Printed in the U.S.A.

Books by Ann Hurley

Silhouette Romance

The Highest Tower #408

Silhouette Special Edition

Touch of Greatness #98
Hearts in Exile #167

Silhouette Desire

Chasing the Rainbow #181
Year of the Poet #233
Catching a Comet #288
A Fair Breeze #321

ANN HURLEY

sprang from a family chock-full of lawyers, teachers and scientists. After a long stint teaching literature and creative writing, Ann realized that she wanted to *write* most of all. Although she has traveled extensively, she chose to settle in Albuquerque, New Mexico, where she frequently walks across the mesa west of the city for a glimpse of the Sandias and the majestic Rio Grande.

One

Leah sat at the rickety kitchen table and mumbled aloud as she wrote out her list. "The gate in front and the fence, the shelves for the pantry...the back steps, the window-frame in my bedroom."

"Everything, in short," her daughter finished, utter contempt curling her lips. "If there was a Board of Health in this town, they'd close the place."

"Look, Fairharbor is not Boston," Leah said wearily without looking up. "That simple fact is the chief attraction for me, Bea Rose. Three months will not—I repeat, not—kill you, but I might. Now, go watch TV or read if you plan to see your eleventh birthday."

From the corner of Leah's eye, she saw ten short fingernails painted a grotesque, cyanotic blue waving at her in derision. She raised her head, returned the horribly bored mask thrust at her with a face of her own and aimed her ballpoint pen menacingly at her only child.

"If I am forced to live here, I'd rather be dead," Beatrice Rose Mackey said with deep feeling. "I miss Daddy and Karen and Beanie already. This house is ugly, the people here are dumb...D-U-M..."

Her recital of complaints faded slowly until it was replaced by a sudden, deafening blast of rock video from the living room. Leah sighed and shouted, without real hope, for Bea to turn it down. She wrote, "Do something with Bea," at the bottom of her list and then crossed it out. The postmistress's nephew could hardly be expected to straighten out more than warped doors and creaking floors.

"Wardwell," a man said loudly from the other side of the sagging screen door.

Leah jumped up, making the coffee slosh in her mug. In the past week, she hadn't been spoken to by anyone but her own daughter, grudgingly, and the birdie little Miss Miranda Murching. She did not count some local who grunted briefly at her when she wished him a good day. Shouldering open the screen, Leah fixed a polite, welcoming smile on her face.

"Come on in, Mr. Wardwell. I was almost ready with my list." She had to raise her voice to be heard. "I'll get you a cup of coffee if you like, while we discuss the work. Bea Rose, turn that down and I mean it. We have company."

There was no adjustment in the noise level, no response from the other room. The man—Jonathon Something Wardwell, Leah believed Miranda called him—stepped inside and glanced once in the direction of the music and back to Leah's face. He surveyed the hideous kitchen in an equal amount of time.

"It's pretty bad," said Leah when he said nothing. "But as your aunt may have told you, we're only renting for the summer. I want it livable, not fully renovated."

She got a nod but no words. He took out a small spiral notebook, a pencil and steel tape measure from the back pocket of his baggy brown pants and walked around the room.

Perhaps ex-husbands and preadolescents were smarter than she gave them credit for, Leah thought as she watched Wardwell. This grand scheme of hers to achieve peace and success had seemed so simple, so perfect in Boston. After one week, she was wondering if Bea was right and the residents of remote coastal towns were largely mutes. And Michael had said that she'd never make a dime on her own or be able to handle people as well as he did.

"We should talk price," Leah announced firmly. "Mrs. Chandler allowed me money for fixing her place up and I'm willing to add some, too, but..."

He came across the torn flowered linoleum right at her, and Leah took a good look at him. He had the typical slouching and unhurried glide of most of the townsmen, young or old. His features were regular and strong but without any expression, his face was average. "Medium" came to mind and the word stuck in Leah's brain. Medium height, weight, with medium blue eyes and medium brown hair. No thrill but no threat.

"Just a minute," he ordered, brushing past Leah. A ship under full speed, he sailed into the living room and the volume suddenly dropped. He was back before the shriek of protest from Bea was over. "Now we can talk, Mrs. Mackey."

"Who? Who?" Beatrice hooted in outrage from the doorway at Leah, gesturing with a peacock blue fingernail at him.

"Jonathon Jericho Wardwell," he said with a suspicion of a smile. "Carpenter by trade and no fan of heavy metal by choice."

Leah sat down at the table, slightly shocked by his presumptuousness but eternally grateful for the quiet. She saw outrage fade from her daughter's flushed face and be replaced by instant curiosity. Slowly, patiently, Jonathon Wardwell was marking down figures in his notebook as if Leah and Bea weren't there.

"I'll do shelving tomorrow," he said. "My advice— save on scrubbing and rip up this floor. I'll sand the wood. It'll be fine—wide plank, I'd guess."

"The cost?" Leah asked shakily. "We have to settle what should be done and what you charge."

"A cup of coffee. Black, please. Little lady," addressing Beatrice Rose, "lend a hand and mark along at the five-foot line on that wall. There's an able child!"

Real shock flooded Leah when Bea actually obeyed, taking the steel tape from Wardwell's outstretched hand and penciling black dots on the far wall. It usually took a catastrophe, like the divorce, to elicit a normal child's response from Bea Rose.

Leah found another mug in the unpacked box of dishes and filled it, preparing to do business. "I assume you don't work just for coffee, Mr. Wardwell. I need figures before I hire you. I understand from Miss Murching you do excellent carpentry, but—"

"This is a nice old house, badly neglected," he interrupted, glancing around once more. "Pity the Chandlers didn't keep it up or get summer folks before."

"We're not exactly tourists," Leah began to explain. "Miss Murching may have told you about the handicrafts cooperative I'm starting in the area for Mrs. Chandler. If she didn't, I'll be happy to—however, first—"

"A well-placed match," suggested Beatrice, obviously recovering her wits. "This dump requires arson, Jon. Our garage in South Shore was bigger and better, believe me."

"Jonathon," he said quietly. "Never Jon, never Jerry. And Mr. Wardwell to most."

Any hint at manners was lost on Bea Rose, as was the warning glance Leah shot at her. "My mother has about as much chance of finding trendy stuff as saving the whales or patching up this haunted house. My father and Karen have a gorgeous new condominium and they think..."

Leah allowed her frayed nerves to part. She had foreseen trouble in uprooting her daughter, even temporarily, from Boston's comfort and amenities. It was impossible to predict the peculiarities of these natives and the unrelenting resistance of Bea Rose. Leah also hadn't foreseen being hit constantly with Michael's dubious wisdom and forty-year-old sarcasm this far away.

"Out!" she insisted. "Remove yourself and that revolting nail polish immediately."

"I would if I could," snapped Bea, "but I can't. Daddy and Karen won't be back until August." She pouted, undoubtedly thinking how much more enjoyable her vacation would be in Mexico with Michael and his new bride, not quite twice her own age, and flounced to her bedroom.

"Sorry," Leah said to Jonathon, feeling sorrier for herself. "She's not overjoyed at the prospects—hers or mine—here."

He sipped once from the mug and stared at Leah over the rim. His eyes looked interested and not unkind to her. "You?"

For some weird reason, that one word made Leah want to cry. Maybe because it was so unusual to be drinking coffee in a kitchen with a man again or maybe because she was too tired, emotionally and physically. She had to blink a few times and examine the oilcloth on the table to maintain her control. She fingered the list she'd made, conscious of his eyes on her. Medium blue, but rather nice.

"I thought...no, I know that we'll be all right here. Katherine...Mrs. Chandler...made me a very good deal with the house and this job tied together. A change of pace and scene is supposed to be... Well, I'm sure you don't want to hear the possible benefits or my plans, Mr....Jonathon."

"I heard some," he said. "Miranda Murching is as good as any town crier ever was. There's not a word you or your girl said that she didn't repeat. You're divorced. Your mister is a rich Boston lawyer with a new missus in tow. You're Maine-blooded and green-eyed, tight with a dollar and you washed the windows the second day you were here. Some of the women think you're too city-proud or young to mix with, but Miranda is all for inviting you for a social. Shall I go on?"

In her annoyance, she forgot he was a stranger and her first visitor. "No, dammit! What kind of place is it where no one talks to you but everybody knows what you ate last night and if you dye your hair?"

He smiled. His amusement startled Leah as much as the gossip had, and he no longer seemed so medium. He had a wonderful, rare smile and it warmed her.

"This is a real small town," he said. "We've got few people and less work, funny ideas and old ways that run about as deep as the ocean. We're largely shy and act cold. And you don't dye your hair."

She couldn't help reaching up and touching her hair, growing out from a chic, expensive cut to dark auburn curls. The gray strands were more obvious the longer it got, and she hadn't bothered to cover them. "Then you can see I'm hardly too young unless there's nobody under thirty-three allowed in Fairharbor."

"Oh, you're allowed. It takes some work to get used to us and let us get used to you, though." He glanced down to scribble a note or two in his notebook, slipping it in his shirt. "I came by to look at you and make you welcome, as well as to find a job. There aren't many true green-eyed people in this world, y'know. Not many I've met, anyway."

When he looked up, his average, solemn face didn't reveal whether he was joking or not. Leah realized that any self-pity and fatigue was gone; he was making her feel a bit edgy and confused. She went to the pot on the stove and held it up, her own version of Fairharbor's nonverbal communication. He gave a similar reply, lifting his cup.

"You're not particularly shy," Leah commented, pouring.

"Or cold," he added, with another brief smile. "I will duly report to Miranda that you do have remarkable eyes, green as Chinese jade, and make an unremarkable cup of coffee. I'll pass on anything else you'd like, as well."

She figured out he was kidding, in a different way than she was accustomed to. He was right about it taking effort to get used to unsophisticated attempts at charm.

"You can spread the word that I'm in the market for any handmade items, arts and crafts," Leah said. "I need all the help I can get and I'm not, contrary to popular belief, too proud to ask."

He stood and Leah was seized with a kind of horror at the thought that he was leaving. If nothing else, she wanted him to stay longer, talk more so she could interact with another adult human being. "Please don't go," she said quickly. "You didn't give me a price on the shelves or any of the other things I need done."

"I take it you've decided I can work for you." He went, easily and slowly, into the living room with Leah following as if he knew the way. "I don't estimate price unless I know how much water the job will ship, Mrs. Mackey. I know you will pay me fairly without us signing articles in dollars and cents. If it's no bother and you feed me, I'll take it off as part of our deal. I can come on board tomorrow morning about six with lumber and nails."

No, not shy, she decided at that instant. Crazy, odd, benignly insane, perhaps, but Jonathon Wardwell was not shy at all.

"Okay, breakfast, but I won't fuss," Leah managed to promise. "Ah, Jonathon, I don't really care about the chimney's condition. It's June."

He was running his hands over the walls, the wooden floor and the fieldstone corner fireplace. He went past Leah, ignoring her, to tap on the treads of the stairs with his knuckles.

"Isn't it lovely how they built such houses?" He patted the carved newel post with affection. "It shows a belief in forever and their future. They expected things to last."

He was sizing her up and making no secret of his appraisal, along with his checkup of the house. She didn't mind, really. It was the kind of open, frank look that had no leer or grab attached.

"I'm less optimistic," Leah said bluntly. "Homes, fortunes and marriages aren't what they used to be. I'll be glad if the house is comfortable while we're in it."

Beatrice Rose came down the stairs wearing silver eye shadow but displaying immaculately groomed, polish-free fingernails for their approval. She waltzed in and out the kitchen and went back upstairs with a glass of milk, without a word.

"How old is she?" asked Jonathon, shaking his head in wonderment.

"Ten," groaned Leah. "But just short of her twenty-fifth birthday. I know! One of the benefits of this move was, hopefully, behavior modification for Beatrice Rose. She's very bright, insightful and incredibly bitter... about life, in general and her lot in same in particular."

"She's not all Yankee like her mother," Jonathon commented. "You've got a bit of a bite to you but you're not scared of much or very defensive. She is, I suspect. Divorced long?"

"Twenty-seven months," Leah replied before she thought about what she was doing. She made it a rule not to talk about the divorce, the nastiness before it and the rough times since. Why on earth would she tell someone she was hiring as a handyman? Why would he ask?

"Do you have a man?" He stood there, one arm draped casually over her banister, made a century before and rented for a summer, and appeared right at home.

"Are you asking for yourself or for Miranda?" Leah countered. She was becoming amused at this man's manner in spite of herself. Why not tell the handyman her personal life? He didn't seem to be making a pass, just gathering information.

"Me. I surmise that the answer is no. Miranda suspects that all divorcées have flocks of men flying in their wake, but she's a romantic-minded spinster."

"Bea Rose and she will have to get together, I see. My daughter's imagination runs to the lurid and passionate, as well."

She hadn't answered Jonathon but he didn't ask her again. Instead, he quickly drained his cup and, assuming a businesslike manner, named an hourly wage that struck Leah as ludicrously low. She wasn't going to argue, however, whether he was being charitable or crazy.

"Tomorrow," she said with a handshake at the door.

"Six o'clock," he promised. "Everyone sails with the tide in Fairharbor, Mrs. Mackey."

"Even us landlubbers?"

She resisted the temptation to glance down at his hand, shaking hers. It wasn't a big hand or heavily callused, as she might have expected. There was firmness to his grip, not mere politeness.

"Don't worry," he said. "You'll both do fine here, you and the girl. This little port here is safe, as well as fair."

Before Leah could say a thing, he was gone, the screen door banging behind him. She heard his footsteps crunching on the coarse gravel and shells of the walk, but the darkness was so complete out here that he was immediately invisible. Even the sounds of his passage vanished quickly, muffled by the sea's distant pulse and the breeze's constant rustle. Still, she stood there and wondered why a stranger's reassurance had pleased her so much.

* * *

Getting up at dawn, as Bea described it, was not their habit. Making a hearty breakfast with eggs and French toast appealed very little to Leah, and eating it at such an ungodly hour even less. Yet there she was, fixing plates and peeking anxiously out the uncurtained window to see if Mr. Wardwell was a punctual self-invited guest.

"Civilized people eat brunch," Bea informed her. "Peasants and farmers rise with the sun, squeeze oranges by hand. Why else did God give us microwaves and frozen foods?"

"Clever," snarled Leah, squeezing another orange dry. "This refrigerator's freezer can store a pint of ice cream and no more. The stove has no griddle in the middle and it does not buzz or light up. Turn that slice over before we find out what charcoal briquettes taste like. He's here. Go let him in, please."

"Yes, master," drawled Beatrice.

Leah knew something was afoot when she heard a yelp of delight from her daughter before Jonathon was even in the house. She ventured a look into the living room and saw him halted at the door, laden with an assortment of tools and a shoulder load of wood. At his feet, Bea was huddled over a cat, stroking the creature's head.

"I smell bacon," Jonathon said cheerfully. "As soon as I'm fed, I'll start."

"French toast, too," Bea volunteered from the floor. "I adore felines. This one has some Persian. What's her name?"

"Not in here," Leah said flatly and she sneezed. "Keep it away from me." There was no need to wait for her allergy to set in; the mere shape of a cat was sufficient.

"Tipsy Jane, I call her." He piled the boards outside the door and stepped over Bea and the cat. "She walks drunkenly from a wound she got in a fight. I can't be putting her ointment on if I'm here, so you can nurse her awhile."

"I won't have a cat," wheezed Leah. "No dog, gerbil, mink or sable, for that matter. I'm deathly allergic to fur."

Bea got up, clutching the largest, ugliest ball of white fur Leah had ever seen. Her mouth was forming a standard protest when Jonathon intervened.

"Take her out to the garden shed in back," he suggested. "Fix her up there. She'll be welcome when the mice come out to play."

"Mice?" Leah shuddered as Bea disappeared with her prize. "There aren't mice, are there?"

"All over." He grinned. "They'll be leaping around the new pantry I'm building you today unless you let the cat prowl. You'll see no whisker or tail if she's here."

Leah was less adamant but unconvinced. She served Jonathon his breakfast while he regaled her with stories of the virtues of cats, on land and sea. She took an antihistamine tablet and joined him on his second round of French toast. Bea was absent after a quick appearance to beat a raw egg into some milk.

"If I so much as see it, it goes," hollered Leah after her. She heard herself capitulating and saw Jonathon's amiable smile confirm it.

"Good thinking," he said, reaching for the margarine. "It'll give her something to occupy herself with, company until she meets the local kids, and it won't be a burden on you."

"It's not that I don't like animals. I'm allergic to them, and she could get attached to this ... Tipsy Jane. I can't take the beast back with us when we leave. As it is, Jonathon, she's been traumatized by separation from her father."

"Fiddle," he said, setting the syrup down with a thump. "It's my cat on loan. Attachment is natural, has to happen, and so does separation. I'm no child psychologist but I think she's bored and lonely. She'll like doing for the cat and the kittens."

"Kittens!" Leah looked at him in stark horror. "The thing is having kittens soon?"

"A week or two, no more."

"No, no, no," Leah said with authority. "I'm going out there and tell her."

Beatrice beat her to the punch, rushing in and flinging herself down into the chair next to Jonathon. She wanted to know where in this wilderness she could find a store that sold cat necessities. "I have an allowance," she said. "My father sends me a check every month. I know my mother won't support a cat."

"And kittens," Leah muttered through taut lips. "Probably hundreds, incredibly hairy."

"Your father must be generous," Jonathon said, keeping his steady gaze on Leah.

"Oh, he is. And Karen takes me shopping with her and buys me the clothes I want. Fashion clothes. I brought some with me, but there won't be anyplace to wear them."

"Leather miniskirts for ten-year-olds," Leah snorted. "Kittens. I have escaped from the frying pan into the fire."

But a cat wasn't as bad as a nineteen-year-old stepmother, Leah thought secretly. It was a healthier interest than some of the pursuits and places that Michael and Karen thought cute or suitable for Bea Rose. There was a world of difference between being precocious and being jaded, she kept telling him.

"All right," groaned Jonathon happily, pushing the plate aside. "I'll kiss the cook and get to work, my dears."

Bea Rose's eyebrows rose and a knowing look crept across her face. She appeared absurdly wise. "Calm yourself," Leah instructed as she cleared the dishes. "Jonathon was not speaking literally. That is a colloquial expression, I'm sure."

He chuckled without agreeing it was. "I'll be taking an hour off later to run to Oliver Peacham's store in Spring Bay, girl. You can ride with me to purchase kitty notions, if you like. Ollie's got masses of children and cats."

"I don't care for many children," Bea said with dignity. "However, I'll go. Jane should have a brush."

Leah was already whipping soap into a froth in the sink and mentally organizing her day. She was unprepared for the arm he slung around her waist, the little squeeze and the contact of his mouth on her cheek. The kiss would have been nothing, a joke, if she hadn't started and turned in his direction at the unexpected touch. But she did swivel her head slightly and they did bump noses and his mouth found hers for a few seconds before they pulled apart.

"Oh, wow," said Bea.

"Thanks for the breakfast," Jonathon murmured politely, taking one step backward.

Leah drew her eyebrows together and frowned, trying to decide whether to say something in front of Bea or pretend it wasn't worth a mention. She did nothing. Her nose tingled and she couldn't rub it with wet hands. The accidental contact had been hard and fast, and she could feel the spot on her lower lip that his teeth, barely cushioned with flesh, had collided with.

She looked over her shoulder at Bea Rose. "I'll call you when I expect help with something. You are at liberty until then, but don't wander off too far."

"Where would I go?" grumbled Bea. "I don't find fish or lobsters particularly exciting except on a menu. Water belongs in a Jacuzzi."

Jonathon was gone from the kitchen, rustling around outside already. Leah finished up the dishes as quickly as possible to let him work alone and undisturbed. At least she told herself that was the reason, while she stayed busy all morning in the other rooms of the house.

It was funny, though, how she kept thinking about the incident. He wasn't nearly as attractive as some of the men she'd been paired off with in Boston, dated, kissed and rejected. A few of them had been downright sexy and reminded her of how terrific it was to be kissed and cuddled and held, how lonely sleeping alone was. But they weren't sexy or appealing enough or she hadn't been lonely enough.

"We're headed out to Ollie's," Jonathon called and stuck his head around the corner. "Want me to pick up anything for you?"

Leah hesitated, wiggling slightly on the stepladder. She brought her arms down from over her head and gripped the top rung.

"No, I'm going past Spring Bay later to see a Mrs. Coffin about her sweaters. Thanks." Leah waited for his head to vanish before she resumed dusting.

He stayed put, the corners of his eyes creased with a squint and a glint no narrowed lids could hide. Leah balanced herself carefully and stood very still, conscious of a very small but significant tensing of her muscles. The sensation lasted only a minute but she remembered it very well, even after all these celibate months. Jonathon saw her as an available woman and her body, acting completely on its own, was reminding her she was. A real woman, she wanted more than clothesline and another gallon of paint. A real live woman was entitled to more.

"I won't be long," he said softly. "Your girl's safe with me, so don't worry."

"I'm not worried," Leah hastily assured him. She was bothered, however. The strange sensation threatened to come back unless she avoided his look and stopped speculating on how competent a carpenter's hands were.

"You've got nice lines, Leah Mackey," Jonathon said. "I can't believe a man would easily give up a woman as trim and well-crafted as you. See you later."

She waited on the ladder until she heard his pickup truck roar off. She didn't feel entirely secure climbing down until then. He'd paid her a simple compliment, that's all, and she was incredibly pleased and inexplicably shaken by it. Thank heavens Jonathon Jericho Wardwell wasn't a mind reader.

TWO

On the coast, they sometimes said a man was "rigged right" and it was the highest compliment possible. If anyone asked Leah, she would have applied the phrase to Jonathon after only a week. Her new shelves were lined with paper and stacked with cans. By midweek, the stove's balky burners were responsive, the front door opened, closed and finally locked. The fence was fixed at a less precarious angle. At this rate, he'd be done with her list in no time.

"More cake?" she pleaded with him. "Do me a favor, Jonathon, and finish it. My hips will thank you."

"There's worse fates than being a broad-beamed woman," he called from the living room, "but bring it out. I'll force myself."

No, Leah couldn't fault his appetite, his work or the man himself. He was always there, it seemed, whether for a few hours or the whole day, but he was never underfoot or in her way. And, miracle of miracles, Bea Rose found him compatible enough to keep a civil tongue in her head, occasionally hand him a tool and to accompany him on a few of his other odd jobs.

Those hours of unbroken, uncomplaining tranquillity were worth as much to Leah as Jonathon's skills. Leah was free to scout out the people who worked wood or carved bone or macraméd.

"Seven exhausting days," Leah muttered, flopping down on the couch. She passed the last of the mocha cake over to Jonathon and pushed off her shoes, curling her legs under her, careful not to encroach on his side.

"You needn't do it all in a week. Rome took longer to build." He began to cheerfully polish off the dessert.

"They had centuries. I've got a few months to make myself indispensable to Kate Chandler and go on to bigger and better things. I see it's going to take a lot of work."

"You're ambitious, I'll say that." Jonathon set the plate aside and brushed crumbs off his jeans. "You rounded up sweaters and wooden toys and got a firm maybe on Arna Templeton's willow baskets. What bargain did you drive to get those things?"

"Three hundred seventy miles and spare change," admitted Leah. "I'm getting to know the area, at least."

His sudden interest inspired her. Generally they spoke only over the meals he took with them—five breakfasts and tonight's dinner, to date—and the subjects were predictably bland. The weather and the day's agenda were standard. There had been no repetition of kissing the cook, no further inquiry into Leah's personal affairs.

"It isn't the mileage I mind," she volunteered. "It's this lengthy process of coaxing and cajoling them to let me see their stuff. Then I spend hours persuading them to produce to order and sell on consignment. You'd think most people don't want the money."

"Oh, they want and need it, all right. There's a big difference, though, in turning out a trinket when it's convenient or marked for a christening, a wedding and promising to whittle five wooden dogs all at once. You talk in terms of a dozen hats knitted in preselected colors, Leah. That's a funny notion to them."

There were plenty of funny things in and around Fairharbor that she still didn't understand. Leah kneaded her eyes with her knuckles and massaged her temples to erase the confusion and irritation inside her. Jonathon was around day after day and until tonight he hadn't once used her first name without adding "Mackey," as if she had a title. He gave her glances that swept over and past her like gentle waves, constant and unfathomable. He told Leah in no uncertain terms that he couldn't work under her supervision and yet appeared to enjoy the company of the ever-critical, smart-mouthed Bea Rose.

"Funny, but who's laughing?" asked Leah. "Elizabeth Coffin could make a whale of an income selling her pretty children's sweaters, more than she's ever seen in one lump sum. But she agreed to two and 'We'll see.'"

We'll see. Whenever she used that phrase on Bea Rose, she got dirty looks. Now Leah understood her daughter's frustration. We'll see if Leah would advance the money for all the yarn or the other materials. We'll see if Mrs. Coffin's sister didn't require several car trips to Boston to visit the specialist, and if Arna's mister's back wasn't acting up and she had the garden filling all her time.

"They're right," Jonathon said, annoying Leah more. "You aren't bargaining with a Picasso who does nothing but paint. A spare-time, busy-hands activity is not their whole art. The art is living and a cellar full of canned summer vegetables is every bit as tempting as cash. They can't eat a sweater or a whittled dog."

"Fiddle," snorted Leah, borrowing one of his favorite exclamations. "Nearly everyone I talked to is old, poor or semiretired. They won't look ahead down the road and risk a little to make a lot."

He objected with a shake of his head. Bea strolled into the room with a nod to Leah and a conspirator's smirk for Jonathon. The cat waddled slowly after her, swollen to enormous proportions.

"What's up?" Leah said immediately. Her nose for secrecy had developed its sensitivity after being blissfully ignorant of so much for too long in her marriage.

Jonathon shrugged and plucked some fluff off the arm of the sofa.

"Oh, nothing," Bea said blithely. "I'm going to bed."

"Willingly? At eight o'clock?" Leah pounced like a tigress on her daughter, feeling her forehead, the glands in her neck. "I told you, didn't I, to wear a jacket in the mornings when it's damp or foggy..."

"I'm fine," whined Bea.

"She's fine," seconded Jonathon. "She's tired from planing the closet doors with me. That, and the walk we took. It's good for children to be tired; they grow at night."

"Yes, tired," said Bea demurely while Leah gaped at her. "Goodnight, guys."

Leah bent down for the ritual kiss and got a juicy one instead, complete with a hug. Now she was sure there was something wrong. "Sweet dreams," she murmured.

Her mouth stayed open an inch or two as her daughter and Tipsy Jane began a stately ascent of the stairs. Bea's manner and show of affection were too startling to raise a puny objection to the cat's presence. Besides, Leah strongly suspected the pregnant beast had been smuggled in the past few nights. She was steeling herself for the blessed event to occur on Bea's floor and realized her sinuses were doomed to kitten dander.

As soon as the bedroom door slammed, Leah hovered over Jonathon. "Tell me everything," she demanded. "Leave nothing out, Mr. Wardwell. What is going on?"

"Nothing harmful," he said quietly. "We were discussing the philosophy of your potential artisans. Well, they believe if a thing ain't broke, you don't fix it. Consider their viewpoint because your daughter's not standing at the harbor, whistling at fourteen-year-old boys. She's fine, I tell you."

Leah's eyes darted to the stairs and back to him. She sat down. "I don't like this one bit and I'm her mother. You've only known her one week, Jonathon; she's up to something. I can feel it in my bones."

"You've got bones that tell tales and hips that thank me," he said softly. "Those aren't standard features, are they?"

"Don't joke. I'm worried!" Leah shook a finger in the air. "She wanders off at odd hours, alone, or happily goes with you to places she wouldn't have sneezed at before, hasn't bought a single torrid supermarket scandal sheet and, it appears, has adopted the terse, closemouthed manner of this whole town when I speak to her..."

Winded, Leah fell back against the cushions and glared accusingly at him. He smiled evenly and unperturbedly, telling her no more.

"She's the proud possessor of fifty dollars, enough to get her back to Boston and her girlfriend, Beanie," Leah said. "Michael sent her *fifty* bucks! He thinks money makes life right, no matter what the problem. She didn't even protest when you referred to her as a child, did you notice?"

"You wanted to see change in her," Jonathon reminded Leah. "Well, change can happen fast here, and change in the young, especially. A tide's turning can be deceptively quick."

"Deception," grumbled Leah, seizing on the word, "is precisely what I'm worried about. I know she's not doing drugs or robbing banks, Jonathon, but I don't know what she is doing lately. She doesn't say much."

"Steady there, Leah." He reached over and took hold of her hand in a slow, deliberate movement. "Why not tell me what's bothering you? Really bothering you. I'm listening."

His gesture and the use of her name, spoken almost as an endearment, stopped her ranting. The road from formality to familiarity was very short, it seemed, but she was not inclined to pull away from him. She had been speculating about Jonathon and his interest in her for a week; part of her wanted to know where this road led.

"I told you already!" Leah exclaimed. "I came here to start over, get some fresh wind in my sails. How do I stand firm, and alone, and on my own two feet, when those winds are potential hurricanes? Bea Rose, the resistance from all these people I've contacted... Michael's insistence on playing Santa Claus, not Daddy..."

She was numbering her troubles with her other hand's fingers and Jonathon captured that one, too, enfolding her woes in his strong grip.

"You can be saltier than the sea," he said. "I sort of like that about you, but I don't like to hear you sound bitter. You're in a hurry to fix your life, but speed isn't what's needed."

"Oh?" She didn't mean to sound cool or tough but there had been too many glib advisers recently. "And you know what I need?"

"Try time and patience and a friend," Jonathon suggested. "I'm offering myself, in case you've missed the point. Me! Do I bother you? I'm finished working here, and I don't want to have to manufacture excuses to hang around."

His touch was friendly. Leah smiled into his eyes, thinking how comforting and warm it was to simply hold hands with him. He smelled like fresh sawdust and mocha cake.

"I think we are friends," she ventured.

"*Becoming* friends," he said emphatically. "You see? There's no hurry or rush to decide if you like me or how much."

"But I *do* like you! There's no big deal, either, in saying it."

He smiled then, and without warning pulled her up against him. His left arm was suddenly around her, the muscular forearm across her back, and Leah instinctively pushed her free hand hard on his chest, her grin vanishing and her eyes wide and wary.

He didn't do anything, but kept smiling for a long, silent minute. Finally he glanced down at her hand and back to her face, so close to him.

"It's a big deal," he contradicted. "I just scared you by hurrying, by doing what a friend might do—hug you."

"I'm not scared. You surprised me." But her pulse was too fast. Her body had stiffened, anticipating a wrestling match. Leah made herself relax slightly, and she fixed a focus on his nose, a less worrisome feature than his mouth.

"Not everything has to be spoken straight out," Jonathon said gently, "but I prefer the plain and simple. If we're going to be friends, let's start with the truth and stick to it."

He took his arm away and Leah stayed put, merely settling herself more comfortably next to him. She wasn't afraid of him or the truth, she reasoned, so why move?

"Okay," she said casually, "fire away. I can't think of any lies I've told. I like you. You're a nice guy, Jonathon. You won't need an excuse to stop by for dinner or coffee when the hammering and sawing is over."

"Good. I'm becoming your friend." He was quiet for a moment and finally tapped Leah on the shoulder until she turned her head back to face him directly.

"I wouldn't mind being your lover, either—not a bit," he said distinctly. "I don't expect it will happen tonight . . . or next week . . . or any special time soon. But I think it will happen. There's certain feelings between us. You know what I mean."

Right to the point and dead on target. She couldn't quite believe anyone could be so blunt and honest yet guileless. She couldn't help staring at him in bewilderment. He'd made a statement, not thrown her a line to test the waters.

"I guess I do," she offered, feeling awkward. "The question I've been asking myself is whether to give those feelings any expression. They've brought me trouble in the past."

He touched the hair at her forehead and in front of her ears. His fingertips brushed her cheek, resting there.

"It's not the feelings that bring trouble," he whispered. "It's who they're attached to. I'm not trouble, Leah."

She tended to agree, was ready to agree, when he slid forward and brought his mouth to hers. There was nothing accidental about his kiss this time, no nose-bumping or mistake.

Jonathon Jericho Wardwell gave her the longest, most thorough and unquestionably best kiss Leah had gotten in ages. It was soft, it was firm, it went on and on, getting deeper and better until she forgot any comparisons and reservations. He didn't hold her, but he didn't have to. Her lips were moving with his; her tongue answered the lingering exploration he made with a subtle assault of her own. The only contact between them was a kiss and the pressure of his leg against hers but her nervous system was screaming, *Trouble!* before he finished.

"Well," he said on a husky little exhalation. "Well, my goodness . . ."

And Leah heard herself make the most embarrassing half giggle, half snort in response. "Yes, it was," she said inanely, and the two of them laughed as if she'd actually been witty.

When they stopped laughing, Jonathon got up, helped himself to two beer from the refrigerator and came back, extending one to her. "I'll drink to that," he said lightly. "I'd do it again, but I know good and well I wouldn't be able to live up to my fine speech about not expecting to make love to you tonight."

"Why, Captain Wardwell," Leah gushed in her silliest Southern Belle imitation, "you do go on! It was just a kiss, you know, and we're big folks."

The way he looked at her made Leah feel like a fool.

"No, it wasn't. It wasn't *just* a kiss," Jonathon said very seriously. "And I'd like to hear you say that before I go home and fantasize some more. I want you, Leah. But I won't let myself want you if I'm only amusing you."

She got off the couch and, taking his hand, pulled him back next to her. "Sorry," Leah said. "That's plain and simple, too. I made it a joke, a brittle and stupid joke, because...because it was so nice and special...and a kiss isn't supposed to mean much nowadays, I've heard."

After a long pull at the beer, Jonathon smiled. "The rule book must be different in Boston. Here, 'you must remember this...'"

She nodded and laughed, singing the next line. "'A kiss is still a kiss, a sigh is just a...'"

A scream? Leah's beer was saved by Jonathon's quick reflexes but her heart froze in midbeat and threatened to crack at a shattering sound from the top of the stairs.

"She's splitting!" Bea Rose shrieked. "Oh, God, Mom, I think the cat's busting or rupturing or something gross."

"City children," said Jonathon with disgust.

"Beatrice Rose, that cat is having kittens," Leah hollered from the bottom step. "Now where is the miserable...Tipsy Jane? On your bed?"

"It's too awful! It's entirely icky," came the wail.

"My sentiments exactly," growled Leah, starting up. "I don't know a thing about birthing babies, Miz Scarlett..."

Jonathon went with her, laughing, and bringing the beer, he said, to fortify the obstetrical team. "It's perfectly lovely, totally natural and highly educational," he told Bea Rose with a reassuring pat on the back. "Come on, we'll give the old thing some moral support and name her fluff balls."

"Sneezy, Wheezy and Redeye," Leah suggested.

Their presence was not really required, but the cat tolerated them, occasionally peeking over Bea's covers when the human conversation and commentary got too loud.

The entire process took only a few hours, but it was sufficient for Bea to be properly awed by what Jonathon constantly referred to as "the miracle of birth."

Leah's more cynical quips, such as "the wages of sin," went unspoken. After the initial fear and trepidation wore off, her daughter's face was a study in unspoiled wonder and amazement. Jonathon made himself comfortable on the rag rug, chatting away as if he attended births every second Tuesday. He discussed old movies with Leah, discovering they shared a passion for the classic cinema, and inviting her to Spring Bay for a Peter Lorre festival.

"Oh, I'd love to," Leah said. "But you know what my schedule's like . . ."

"She hates dates," Bea Rose interrupted. "Says she feels like the world's oldest teen and it's the silliest social custom invented."

"Well, it is," Leah insisted, seeing Jonathon grin. "It's artificial, stilted, a ritual with no—"

"Then, it's settled. Friday, I'll make you dinner, for a change, and we can overdose on subtitled German films that will break at all the best parts and flicker wildly."

"Well, I'll think about it."

"Six!" crowed Bea Rose. "Oh, Jonathon, why is she getting up? Doesn't she want them?"

"Her legs need a stretch. She's done. I better stretch and go myself or I'll never have the strength to tackle your porch and some cabinets over in Kildear tomorrow."

Leah glanced at the digital clock and noted that it was tomorrow. Three-twenty in the morning and no one had slept. She offered the couch to Jonathon and half her bed to Bea until they could coax Tipsy Jane to set up her nursery in a better spot. Bea yawned once and disappeared down the hall; Jonathon looked vaguely troubled.

"You're letting yourself in for more talk," he said, while Leah piled his arms with pillows and a blanket. "I just want you to know before you get the evil eye at the supermarket."

"I always wanted to be thought of as wicked," Leah said with a wink. "The new Siren of Fairharbor will set the clock for six-thirty."

"You don't have to." Jonathon dumped his bedding and turned to hold her shoulders. "I won't sleep. Not with you upstairs, not with imagining how much I'd like to give certain rumors a foundation in truth. Think about being wicked with me; I will."

Leah put her arms around his neck and gave him a very chaste, brief good-night kiss. She was going to tell him she was ripe for revolution but not romance when he returned it, holding her tight to himself, making their mouths meet and part and meet once more. The heat and feeling of his body against hers was enough to make her forget her speech; the kiss conjured up a very vivid picture of where else his mouth would delight her.

"Good night, Jonathon," she whispered, drawing back. "And I refuse to believe you have a wicked bone in your body."

"If you had held on a little longer, I would have shown you," he said, "like it or not."

The supermarket posed no problem for Leah. Miranda Murching's post office, however, was a hotbed of steamy whispers and arched eyebrows. There was always a crowd of women, never a line. The men tended to congregate in the sporting goods store next door to keep their gossip separate from "ladies' tiddle-taddle."

"Uncle Ephraim, who lives with us, carves driftwood buttons," a woman informed Leah. "I heard you'd be interested."

"Only if she's as dotty as your uncle," said Miranda from her counter. "Ninety-two, isn't he? A perfectly dreadful old man."

"They're lovely buttons...a trifle big to be practical," the woman went on. "He started on soap..."

"He can't fashion anything smaller than a wagon wheel," Miranda added. "He lost his buttons years ago. That's why he makes 'em."

"I really don't think there's much of a market..." struggled Leah, trying to control herself. "A book of stamps, please, Miranda, and three postcards." She handed her mail over and waggled her own eyebrows at Miranda.

"Now, you take Jonathon, my nephew..." Miss Murching announced loudly.

"Hasn't she?" came a stage whisper from somewhere behind Leah.

"He's a craftsman. He's an artist," the postmistress said fiercely. "My sister was clever with her hands, I'll say that. But Jonathon Jericho has positive genius. Doesn't he? And he would set his cap for someone who'd appreciate him fully, wouldn't he?"

Conversation in the room ceased. Leah realized she was being directly addressed. No one wanted to miss her answers, obviously.

"He's got magic in his fingers. I've never seen him wear a hat," Leah said in her best Fairharbor style.

Miranda looked over the top of her glasses sharply, and there were a few chuckles at the outsider's neat side-stepping of the real question.

"You took my meaning, Mrs. Mackey. He talks of nothing else but you and your girl. He's over there pretty near every day..."

"And a night," a woman's muffled alto tacked on.

Leah spun around, but there was no one with an open mouth to accuse. "This is not the time or place, Miss Murching, to discuss your nephew," she said, confronting the old lady. "And it's not anyone's business, besides."

"Of course it is. When the best bachelor around is pushing thirty-seven, we'd all like to see him securely anchored and flying some decent colors. He ought to be married and replenishing the earth. He should be recognized by someone for the artist he is. If he's fixed on your star, we'd like to hear so we know where he's heading."

The woman who ran the Laundromat bustled up and took Leah's elbow. "Well, I, for one, don't care who does what to who or why. Go see my sister, Clare. She and this hippie from Vermont are living together behind Jack's gas station on Cove Road. He makes pots, so you might like them."

"No one else does...like them or his pots," clarified another brave soul. "I'd take Wardwell and his ships over the Green Mountain man and his greenware any day."

"Shut up! You're married and not in the running," the Laundromat lady ordered. "You just tell Clare, Mrs. Mackey, that I said it was okay to talk to you."

"What's your name? Cove Road? What ships?" muttered Leah, scribbling furiously on a certified mail receipt.

"Helen Ellison. Pleased to meet you. Stop by Suds 'n' Duds, why don't you?"

"It's getting to be a crime, I guess, to be married," snorted the rebuffed woman to everyone in general. "I've got a license, not a lease, with my old man. More than some can say!"

The alto from the back trumpeted again. "We know your Tom. You ain't saying much, Edna. I would have leased and vacated long ago."

"I got a cheaper license with my dog...and a better deal" came from a corner.

Uproarious laughter greeted every comment. Leah stuck the directions in her purse and looked around, baffled. Miranda Murching had her elbows propped on the counter and her chin daintily poised on her hands, taking in—and loving—each sally.

"Best show in town," she said to Leah. "I'll never retire if they don't make me. Beats hell out of watching soap operas, doesn't it?"

"I'm not sure," admitted Leah. "Rather vicious sport."

Miranda dismissed the idea with a wave. "Pooh! No malice at all. Everyone knows everything, anyway. Gives us a chance to poke fun and get stuff off our chests."

As if to prove the point, Edna was delivering her final round. "Say, *I* didn't have any ten-pound premature baby, Alice Barnstable. I can tell you that!"

The alto, a heavyset brunette, strolled up, instantly and forever identifying her as Alice Alto in Leah's mind. Instead of scowling or appearing ready to scratch and bite, she was laughing. "I didn't say that Kelly was premature. I will say the wedding was a tad late, however!"

When the post office was relatively calm again, Leah asked Miranda about the ships someone had mentioned. She hadn't forgotten the reference in the chaos that followed.

"Oh, you'll see them Friday," Miranda said. "Which reminds me...have Bea Rose trot down for dinner about

six. We'll want plenty of time to see both the movies I
rented for the VCR.''

"Miss Murching, I didn't even ask anyone to baby-sit
Beatrice Rose. How in the world did you know about
Friday?''

"She and I made our own plans," Miranda replied with
a chuckle. "We've got two good ones, too. *Valley of the
Dolls* and—"

"Spare me," groaned Leah, fleeing as fast as she could.

"He won't sell them," Miranda called to her. "Don't
bother to ask ... Six sharp, tell her."

"I buy crafts," Leah said, as if reassuring herself. "Not
small craft. I don't care if Jonathon Wardwell can build
cruisers out of toothpicks."

Three

———

Fairharbor was really composed of two villages. There was a lower town circling the harbor and an upper ring nestled in the hills and on granite bluffs. It was a step into social history as well as geography and, on the way to his home, Jonathon enlightened Leah. As far as she could see, there were no striking differences; the houses, up or down, were basically indistinguishable to her and Fairharbor was one place.

"Same size houses, white or gray or tan," she said, "unless you're counting the bigger gardens near me or the fancier weather vanes."

As he turned his pickup down a street, he gestured out the window at the harbor's warehouses and gear shacks a scant block away. "Chandler House is high class, on the hill. A ship's pilot or a captain must have built it. The lowly hand, fisherman and humble merchant lived beneath those sorts, with the sea lapping the front door and their ankles. A captain wanted the wind in his hair and a clear view of the harbor all the time.''

She surveyed his neat Cape Cod, freshly painted, gleaming white in the twilight. There were window boxes filled with marigolds and cascading petunias. Every flagstone on the tiny path beyond the fence might have been hand polished. His yard made her riot of untrimmed hedges and scraggly, leggy flowers at Chandler House look like a slum.

''Hey, some carpenter—or ship's carpenter—puts me to shame,'' she kidded. ''Are you, or your historical counterpart, considered low class?''

She was hoping Jonathon was in one of his talkative moods. When he was at the house, it didn't matter if they talked or not. There, she was comfortable with him, not at all nervous. The efficient motion of his hands, the sounds of each job taking shape while he was sawing and filing and hammering occupied her. He always kept a half smile on his face, taking pleasure in the work, and conversation was easy.

Tonight she was skittish. Friends or not, they were out together, a man and a woman. Dating complicated matters, and she was after the simple life, wasn't she?

''I'm not sure whether I'm low class or not,'' Jonathon said, laughing. ''Poll around town for opinions, if you like. As for a ship's carpenter, it depended entirely on how good he was. Some men were only fit for making coffins and boat hook handles. There were a few who could assemble a new ship out of a wreck to sail the survivors home. A carpenter was more of a necessity, taken for granted. He wasn't heroic or famous, just good or bad, and he had to be there.''

That's you, she was tempted to say. She was beginning to take his presence for granted, while appreciating how much of a necessity he had become. Whatever he did, he did as well as he could, with a minimum of fuss, and everything got done.

"Oh, this is lovely!" Leah went around the living room, admiring his tasteful, beautiful decor. "You better keep a sharp eye on me, Jonathon. I'm stuck with overstuffed Early American bargain basement and you've got real antiques."

"Help yourself," he offered cheerfully, going to the kitchen. "The brass and wood take nothing but hours and hours of polishing. Sit on those ladder-back chairs half an hour and you'll know why old portraits are always frowning."

She saw it then. There was a ship in a shadowed corner on a walnut drum table. Like a homing pigeon, Leah flew across the rug, searching for another lamp to fully illuminate the huge model.

Her lack of knowledge about sailing ships, real or model, didn't diminish her excitement; she recognized authentic art and knew genuine craftsmanship inside out. Without daring to touch or lift it from its wooden stand, Leah stood in awed contemplation of a nearly four-foot-long ship. The tall, straight spars were hung with a web of intricately organized and looped threads, as delicate and precise as a spider's best effort. The perfection of detail, the order of seemingly thousands of fittings and pieces, the ship's clean lines were breathtaking.

"The *Jericho*," said Jonathon, from behind her. "As in Jonathon Jericho Wardwell. She's a clipper, one of the queens of the sea, but she didn't sail. She was never built, actually, until I made her from the original plans."

Leah exhaled loudly. "Wow, to borrow Bea's every other word. Wow! A model... I usually associate model ships with those kits of plastic pieces to punch out and

glue, with plenty of decals slapped on every which way.
This...it's...I mean, she's a museum piece. How long
does it take you to make one? Why isn't it...she pro-
tected in a glass case? Where are the sails?"

"Whoa," he ordered, taking her elbow. He steered
Leah toward the dining room table while her head stayed
resolutely craned back over her shoulder. "You're going
to be sorry you're asking questions. Once I get wound up
on clippers, I won't stop until your forehead slumps into
the mashed potatoes."

"Go ahead," she urged. "Tell me. I'll wave my napkin
to signal when I've had enough."

Miranda had warned her not to ask, but it was impossible not to speculate on the price a Boston store would
ask for such a handmade treasure. Two thousand, twenty-
five hundred was her first calculation.

Jonathon carved the roast and filled her plate. "It takes
me fifty to two hundred hours just to make a hull," he
said nonchalantly. "I don't keep actual records on how
long I work on them. It's not important."

Them. More than one. Leah's brain clicked, registering the enormous amount of labor. *Thirty-four to four
thousand dollars, say. A yacht club would kill to have
one.*

She should have complimented his cooking or mentioned the novelty of having a man make her a dinner, but
instead she chewed mechanically and pointed at an old
engraving on the wall. The ship in the print was under full
canvas, like outspread wings, and skimming over the
waves.

"No glass case; that's for exhibits where someone's
likely to mess the rigging," Jonathon said, covering her
string of questions. "And I believe it's ludicrous for a ship
out of water to have set sails. It's an unnatural monstros-

ity, although I know plenty of model builders do it. If the *Jericho* could sail, she'd have her canvas.''

He was a purist and an historian. She should have known. While she ate the main course, Leah heard about the *Flying Cloud*, a famous clipper, including the name of her designer of 1851 and the ship's remarkable record voyage to San Francisco in eighty-nine days. Jonathon also recited the speed, the captain's name, the clipper's complete record of service until a fire gutted the ship. His enthusiasm was contagious and her ignorance was vast, Leah freely admitted.

"Anyone around here could tell you this stuff," he said modestly, when she oohed and aahed. "There's even one or two old men who might actually know how to sail one." He sighed and cleared the table, refusing to let her lift a finger. "I hate to say it, but I almost wish the Age of Steam hadn't taken over. There would still be a fleet of the most beautiful, graceful vessels ever invented. And the *Jericho* would be real, a historic item in books with footnotes and not a pretty dust catcher."

Leah disregarded his instructions and followed Jonathon into the kitchen, colliding ungracefully with him when he stopped suddenly. "Oh, no! Don't say that! Your ship is a masterpiece in its own right. Oops, sorry... I wanted to hear the *Jericho*'s history and why you're named for it."

He shook his head and cut thick slabs of pie. Leah shook her head and clutched her stomach in mock agony. Jonathon grinned broadly and took in two plates, anyway.

"You're drooling," he said. "You must want pie. It better be the pie, Leah Mackey, because you aren't getting any other treats from me."

"I didn't ask, now, did I?" she said sheepishly, pushing the plate to one side. Her greed might as well have been a neon sign blinking over her head.

He ate a few forksful and let her stew. The blueberries left a smudge at the corner of his mouth, and Leah jabbed at her face until he got the idea and wielded his napkin.

"I expect I might have gotten a dribble kissed away if I played my cards right," he said breezily. "But I didn't and I'm not going to. I'm sure Miranda blabbed. I would have shown the ships to you eventually. They're not for sale, though."

"Okay, I hear you," lied Leah. It was not okay. She saw herself waltzing into Kate Chandler's office, the *Jericho* or another like it in her arms, and the elegant Ms. Chandler spouting praise, begging her to run the new gallery, name her own salary.

"I'm working on another Donald McKay design, *Lightning*, right now." Jonathon checked his watch. "I'll show her to you, if you like. We'd better hurry or we'll be late for the movie."

"Which Wardwell designed the *Jericho*? Grandfather? No, great-grandfather. Or was it mother's side?"

"Great-great," he supplied. "They married, bred and died earlier in those days. Josiah Windham Wardwell is the name you're seeking and you won't find him in any history texts, either. The poor fellow spent most of his life trying to outdo McKay and the great British builders. He came up with a crown jewel at the precise moment in time when no one wanted it. No investors, no money, no *Jericho*."

"So it was never built," Leah summed up. "Must have been a bitter disappointment."

Jonathon led her into his workroom, snapping on the overhead fluorescent lights and let her enjoy prowling and peeking around for a few minutes. He didn't speak until he plunged the room into darkness again and his voice was soft, regretful.

"Josiah killed himself. It's a melodramatic touch I hate in books but true. His business was thriving but not renowned. From his letters and diary, I gathered his family adored him and he was surrounded with friends and admirers. He couldn't stand not being the best, what it amounted to, and the best was measured through other people's eyes. He didn't trust his own estimation, a common failing."

"It's tragic," agreed Leah as they got ready to leave. "But you know, I can understand the man's despair. How can you feel like the best or be sure you are the best, until you can demonstrate it? The *Jericho* might have put every other clipper to shame, broken the records for speed and dazzled every eye, but he'd always have to wonder."

"I don't wonder. She was flawless, the best," said Jonathon tersely. He locked the front door and walked to the truck, lost in deep and private thoughts.

Leah didn't intrude. She was too busy with her own ideas, hatching and discarding improbable schemes to persuade Jonathon to sell her one of the models. She reviewed everything he'd said, trying to reconcile what she'd found out with what she observed about him. The lure of money alone wasn't going to snare him; he seemed to be content and lived comfortably. She could hear Michael's all-purpose maxim, "Everyone has his price," bouncing around inside her head as they bumped along the rough blacktop.

All right, she decided with unshakable resolve, a bargain could be struck. Fame, riches, glory, success... whatever it was, she'd find the price and be the consummate Yankee trader. If Jonathon Jericho Wardwell wanted publicity or recognition for his ancestor's dream, there were magazines and papers, especially in New England, that would gladly pick up his story.

"Hello? Lost in the parade?" she asked when Jonathon parked and sat staring blankly at the tiny marquee. "Did you change your mind about the show?"

He came out of his reverie and pocketed the keys, leaning across the worn upholstery to plant a quick kiss on her cheek. "Not at all. Sorry, I'm not really moody, just wool-gathering."

"Any special sheep?"

He smiled. "I'm not sure you'd like to know, and if you knew, I'm not sure you'd like it. I was thinking about you."

"Care to be more specific?"

"Later," Jonathon said and looked hungrily at her.

The touch of his voice registered. The impact and feeling of his eyes on her sunk in. For a few seconds, the lights on the theater marquee swam and blurred, and Leah experienced a terrible throb of desire, brief but hot and blatant. The intensity of it shocked her and made her feel shaky when he came around to help her out. The invisible pulse lasted even after they went in and sat down. Leah was trying hard to hide a lusty secret she thought of as both adolescent and exciting.

She wanted him. She kept her eyes on the screen, waiting for her mind to protest and reject the realization. Instead, all she could see was his face, intense with passion and intent on her. Whenever Jonathon shifted his body, she heard "later" over the harsh German sound track and remembered how his mouth felt the other night. She wanted him to touch her.

Every once in a while, Jonathon turned to look at her, especially when their hands linked at a tense moment or their legs made contact. He didn't put his arm around her or whisper any comments in her ear but, oddly enough, his careful behavior, his almost shy distancing of himself was arousing her more.

She loved the movie for the umpteenth time, but she wasn't sorry when the house lights flicked on. It was nice to have something more to look forward to; she felt good to want and be wanted again.

"Nobody was creepier than Lorre," Leah said as they emerged from the little theater. "Richard Widmark did great psychopaths but, boy, I got the willies tonight."

He slung an arm casually around her shoulder and hugged her. "You should have worn a sweater. It's the evening air."

"I saw you jump a few times," Leah teased as they climbed into the truck. "My palm wasn't the only sweaty one when he was cornered in the cellar."

"It was holding hands. Always makes me nervous," Jonathon said. "I was afraid you'd finish all the popcorn, and I'm not as dexterous with my left alone."

They joked and bantered back and forth on the drive home with an ease Leah always associated with long acquaintance. Her description of her encounter with the Cove Road hippie and Helen Laundromat's sister delighted Jonathon.

"There are more eccentrics per square mile in New England than anywhere else," he said with a chuckle. "Everyone thinks the rugged individualists all went West. They should meet Miranda Murching and Oscar Peavy and a few more than you've encountered lately."

"Charlie Cranberry," snorted Leah. "He's legally changed his name to Cranberry. Now if he could throw a pot that didn't leak or crack or look like the Leaning Tower of Pisa, I might be able to sell his stuff."

"Another wild-goose chase, huh? You ought to drive down to Wilder Bay and see if Art and Emma are still alive and kicking. They used to dig their own clay and make those things. A funny old couple."

"Boy, you're a gold mine!" exclaimed Leah. "I should have pumped you for information instead of the post office gang. But I didn't expect much encouragement from a fellow who wouldn't even discuss his own craft with me."

"I discussed it," Jonathon said shortly. "I just won't sell it."

"Which I chalk up to another major eccentricity," added Leah snidely.

"Call it what you like." He parked and set the brake.

Leah had her hand on the door handle but hesitated. They weren't in front of his house. She recognized the approach to Miranda Murching's drive. She had assumed "later" meant alone, at his house. It obviously meant cuddling at the Chandler House with Bea Rose and the kittens tucked in for the night.

"I'll go get her," Leah started to say, but his arm got to her first. After a lingering kiss, she had no inclination to go at all.

Jonathon always took his time, it appeared. He carefully fitted his mouth to hers, brushing and nibbling her lips, while his hands slid her closer and closer until they were bound together in the vise of his grip. He tasted salty from the popcorn but hot and sweet from a flavor all his own, and Leah let him know she liked his kisses, wanted to taste much more of him.

It was gloriously easy to melt and be absorbed into the solid heated feeling of his cradling arms, his hard, warm chest. Leah's hands stroked up his neck into his hair, silky between her fingers. Against the softness of her breast, she felt the rapid beating of his heart, a tempo as fast as her pulse, her own breathing.

"Jonathon . . . I thought you meant—"

"Don't think," he interrupted. "I like to hear you say my name, but let's talk later." After a few more kisses, she did whisper breathlessly, "Jonathon . . ."

"It's going to be good for us," he whispered back. "Wonderful. The best." He gave her no chance to reply, his mouth seeking hers once more.

Leah made a sound of agreement, half-buried in her throat, and clung to him, returning kiss for kiss, allowing her hands to measure the breadth and strength of his back. There was too much clothing, too little space in the truck but if he wanted to make love to her right here and now, she was almost willing to try.

His hands were driving her crazy, lightly outlining the shape of her breasts under the blouse. He kept running his fingertips around the cloth, plucking at the hard nipples, rubbing them gently until Leah was afraid she would scream. Once or twice, his hands slipped under the fabric to cup and tease her more, the rougher skin of fingertips and palms caressing her as if she was velvet and his thumbs delicately flicking more and more life into the taut, aching tips.

His lips lifted, found her ear, but his fingers kept busy. "I dreamed they were dark, mahogany dark and more red right here . . . and not very large but so sensitive when they're hard this way. And I hoped you would want me to kiss them as much as I wanted to . . . that you would ask me to do whatever you wanted . . . Will you?"

"Yes," breathed Leah, feeling weak and hollow with desire. "I'm afraid to ask what else you pictured . . ."

"Are they?" His thumb and forefinger rolled one of her nipples lightly, sending a long shudder through her. "Dark and sensitive? I'll use my mouth, my fingers... whatever will give you the most pleasure."

"Yes, yes," she gasped, the sound swallowed in the deep, wild kisses he gave her. His mouth was moving frantically but his hands stayed tender, a combination of sensations that made her hips yearn to move under his.

"Oh, Leah," he murmured hoarsely, slowly breaking the seal of lip and body, "Leah, you were worth the waiting... the dreaming. I'll stop until I can match all your reality to my fantasy. Until I can love you the whole night and all the time."

Don't stop, she was ready to say. She had waited centuries to come alive again, for the fierce longing for a man to return. When? she wanted to ask. But the blaze of intensity in his moonlit eyes was determination, not merely need. She touched his mouth, feeling its wonderful shape that promised so much, and her fingers detected the set, tight line of his jaw and cheek.

"I can give you the whole night," Leah said very quietly. "I wouldn't mind you being my lover, not a bit."

"When it's right, I will be."

"And is 'right' on a calendar, printed in red, right after Saturday or before Tuesday?"

Even as she spoke, the strangeness of the situation hit her full force. She'd fended off men who insisted they were right for each other and attraction alone was what made a night together imperative. Jonathon spoke as if an affair was inevitable but acted as if it wouldn't happen.

"We'll know when it's right," Jonathon said. "We'll know if it's real."

Sense replaced sensation in her. He was saying he wasn't sure. Well, neither was she. She'd come here to heal, not to hurt or be hurt. She could toss around words like "aggressive" and "assertive" with the best of her friends, but the context was always business, not pleasure.

"All right, Jonathon," she agreed, opening the door for herself. "We'll play this by ear, if that's what you're saying."

Getting out hurriedly, she nearly missed his reply. Hearing it, she froze, unable to say or do anything.

"I'm not playing. I think I love you."

A dull ache began inside her chest. She took a deep breath and let it out little by little until the pain went away. Her eyes closed, blocking out the moon, the stars, the glow of the single street lamp. *Too soon,* her heart thudded dully. *Not now.* But *not you* did not sound the expected warning.

They walked up Miranda's driveway, practically but not quite touching, and neither of them said anything. Leah lifted her fist when there was no answer to the bell and was horrified to see the tremor in her hand. She should be flattered, if anything, not frightened.

"Why, Leah! Jonathon! How nice," Miranda gushed, pushing her eyeglasses up on her nose. "I'll put on tea, or would you rather have a snort? I've got a wine so dry, it came as a powder, not a liquid."

"Miss Murching," said Leah huskily, "we're here for Bea Rose. Bea Rose! *Valley of the Dolls*?"

"She would have loved it," Miranda said, throwing the door wide open. "But it's too late to rerun it now! Sakes, she should be in bed. Well, where is she?"

Leah put her hand on the woodwork for support. "She's here, Miranda. She's supposed to be here!"

"Oh, no," said the postmistress loudly, and then she repeated herself more softly. "Oh, no. She popped by the post office this afternoon and told me you changed your mind and you were taking her with you. Yes, yes, that was it!''

"What was she wearing?" Jonathon asked, and when Leah stood there, dazed, he pushed her into the house.

"And you didn't check with me?" Leah blurted out, grabbing Miss Murching's hand. "Omigod, that was five hours ago! Jonathon, I have to get to the house! Right now!"

He was already dialing the phone and held it out to her. "Tell Ray what she was wearing and how much money she had with her. We'll swing by Chandler House and go right to the highway just in case she decided to hoof it or hitchhike."

"Hitchhike!" Leah grabbed the receiver with fingers that had no feeling, talking with lips that felt carved from wood. "If she did . . . Jonathon, if she isn't dead, I'll kill her if she hitchhiked . . ."

"Oh, my," said Miranda Murching, "I'm going to find my brandy. And three big glasses."

"This is Leah Mackey, Ray. Yes, the new lady. . . Ray, I'm calling about my daughter. . ." She heard a stranger talking, calm and composed, while she could feel her insides begin to shred, to tear and bleed.

Jonathon put his big hand gently on her shoulder.

Four

One stop," Jonathon insisted. "I have to check something."

Leah sat rigid, holding panic at bay, while he left the truck and darted down one of the harbor wharves. She heard the slapping sound of his running feet. He was only gone a few minutes, but it felt like an hour before he got back, panting and looking somewhat relieved.

"It's okay. My skiff's still there," he said, gunning the engine and pulling away. "She's on foot, in a bus or a car."

"What do you mean?" demanded Leah icily, clutching his upper arm. Her mind was racing faster than the truck's motor. "A boat? Of course, she wouldn't take a boat. She doesn't know anything about boats. Jonathon?"

He shrugged her hand off and kept his eyes on the narrow streets leading to the hill. "Yes, she does. That was

her big secret! I taught her how to row like every kid in
Fairharbor. She was going to show off for you and be able
to row from the harbor to the point by next weekend. Said
she wanted me to build her a skiff of her own, tailor-
made, and she'd help me out—plane the doors, pull
weeds, grocery shop."

"Beatrice Rose said *that*!" A high, strident note
squeaked out and Leah quickly trapped it. "And you believed her? A child whose idea of physical labor has been
walking to the corner mailbox or mixing martinis for her
father? Oh, God..." She groaned and held her head.
"She's not at the bottom of the Atlantic yet, you mean."

"She did real well," Jonathon said simply. "She rowed
alone every morning last week and kept her bargain with
me."

"And now she's run away." The reality was catching up
with her.

"Not because she learned to row," he said, glancing at
Leah.

"You're absolutely right," Leah said throatily. "What
you did or didn't do isn't the issue. Bea's my problem, and
this mess is my mistake. I insisted she spend the whole
summer here with me, not swinging through Mexico with
Michael and his new bride. I yanked her out of her natural environment, not you. I think she was trying to adjust
and couldn't!"

"You're pretty hard on yourself," commented Jonathon. "I'd wait and see what her explanation is, when
she's back."

"If she's back..." moaned Leah and clamped her teeth
tightly together. There were no lights glowing in the house
as they drove up. She flung herself out and was fumbling
with the well-oiled lock immediately.

Racing through the house, Leah found only the kittens, mewing, and no evidence that Bea had left with more than she was standing up in. She came back to Jonathon with a slower step and her head hung in dejection.

"Where is she? And why? Why did she run?" Her head felt too heavy to lift; her eyes wandered unfocused along the floor. "I would have understood this more if it happened when the divorce was going on . . . her fears and uncertainty . . ."

Jonathon hugged her, rocking her slightly in his arms. He rested his head on the top of hers. "I don't know. You don't know. Maybe even your daughter doesn't know. But right now, the important thing is to find her. I'll look around."

The lights in the living room flickered, and Leah started at a long, rolling peal of thunder. She tore herself from Jonathon's embrace and rushed to the windows.

"Okay, I'm leaving," Jonathon announced. "You call everybody you can think of around the area and pump them for information. It'll help Ray and his deputy, if anyone saw her this evening. There's a few places, a couple of coves, I want to check out."

"It's raining," Leah said morosely, watching the fat drops begin to spatter on the glass. She let the curtain fall. "We used to stand outside and count the intervals between the thunder and the lightning. Bea could tell how far away the storm was. I'll go with you. No, I'd better stick near the phone."

"Yeah, you stay and wait to hear something. Leah, she probably didn't get far, and if we get a squall, she'll head indoors."

She nodded, unable to talk. The terrible possibilities were too scary and too many to verbalize, and she refused to allow herself the luxury of breaking down until a crisis was over. There was no need for Jonathon to drive around on bad roads in bad weather; Michael would have said the police, the proper authorities, could handle their own job and take over. But she was absurdly grateful for Jonathon's offer.

He was already out the front door when Leah ran after him. The wind was cruel, driving sand and rain into her face, and the temperature had dropped abruptly. Leah called loudly, intending to tell him that he shouldn't spend a whole night searching. When Jonathon rolled down the window, unable to hear her above the wind's shrieking, she was struck speechless.

He stuck his hand out and gave her numb fingers a hard squeeze. "I'll call you every couple of hours, whether I've found her or not. You might have heard something and I just want to make sure you're doing all right. Go get busy on the phone; it'll leave less time to worry."

"Thanks," she croaked and stepped back. After the truck vanished down the road, she tacked on, "...friend," and accepted the chaotic jumble of emotions rising in her as unavoidable.

He was a friend but also more. For an instant as brief and dangerous as a pastel lightning spike, Leah thought of love. *Gratitude*, she amended, wrapping her damp arms around her middle. *Gratitude and longing and loneliness. And a healthy dose of desire.*

Right now, love was as much a luxury as collapsing from worry and fear. She couldn't afford either. Dry-eyed but thoroughly soaked, Leah went back in and set to work. With jerky, mechanical motions, she ran through the short directory for Fairharbor and neighboring villages, marking and calling those Bea Rose knew by sight or name. The list was as slim as her chance that her daughter had simply skipped off to a different place for the night, neglecting to mention the fact or get permission.

"Right, Ollie, about six. No? Well, I didn't think so, but thanks. Okay, I'll wait." She twisted the cord around her hand while the Spring Bay storekeeper went to wake his children, ask a few questions and return. "I'm sorry, too. But if you should...

"Thanks."

After Jonathon called with nothing hopeful to report, Leah dug out her address book and dialed Boston. Anyone Bea Rose might remotely consider visiting was rudely wakened, crudely interrogated. It turned out to be a two-pot-of-coffee job with aspirin chaser—frustrating, humiliating and, worst of all, fruitless. Had Bea called there? Was she there? Would they let Leah know the second she showed up? And yes, she was miserably aware that it was three-thirty in the morning.

As she stuck the address book away, a slip of paper fluttered out. Leah took Michael's itinerary, hotels and dates neatly printed by his secretary, wadded it and threw it aside. It was highly unlikely Bea Rose could make it across the border on fifty dollars. The idea of notifying him was rejected before it ever took root.

To Michael an emergency meant a foreclosure, an investigation of the Securities Commission or a detail about a firm's liability. Michael Mackey was the last person to call for support or aid. He never had been, she realized after the divorce. A child's fever, a broken car or heart were minor troubles of daily existence; such complaints annoyed him and bogged down his work. Michael always liked to hear how something was resolved, not about the conflict.

"It's me," said Jonathon on a static-filled line. "The storm's terrific north of Fairharbor. How are you holding up?"

"Fine," she lied and repented immediately. "Well, less than fine. I should have let Miranda get me drunk."

"Hang in there," ordered Jonathon. "When this is over, I'll buy us a liquor store and a steak dinner."

"You've got a deal," Leah said weakly. He sounded so optimistic, as if he'd gone out to find an open store for a quart of milk.

She hung up and paced. No clinic or hospital for a hundred miles had bad news. The train and bus stations had no good news; no one had seen a slim girl with a magenta scarf tied around her head, tan Windbreaker over a Prince T-shirt and bright orange high-topped sneakers. Bea Rose was traveling light, alone and conspicuous.

The thunderstorm was the summer variety, swift and violent but short-lived. The whole house reverberated with booming noises until Leah's uneasiness reached the breaking point. She coaxed the cat downstairs and carried the cardboard carton with nested kittens along, willing to risk asthma for the presence of other life.

She accused herself, with Tipsy Jane as witness, of not being tough enough, hard enough, when a human child could do as she damned well pleased. Her moods swung wildly from fury to misery and despair. She had been too tough, too strict, she thought, in an effort to balance Michael's total permissiveness.

Every time the telephone rang, Leah could feel the surge of fear like a cold wave washing over her. It was exhausting to stay above it, and eventually she dozed fitfully on the couch, next to the phone. The majority of the calls as the day wore on were from Fairharbor people, inquiring anxiously for news, offering suggestions. As much as she wanted to scream and slam the receiver down in frustration, their concern touched her.

Over and over, they asked what they could do, virtually begging to be given some trivial task to help out. She refused the frequent offers of company or food, knowing soon she would not be civil or sane enough to have another person nearby.

Jonathon's calls were different. He was as tired as she was, from the sound of his voice, but he called regularly, refusing to give up his personal search. And Leah could almost believe his calm, low assurances that everything was going to be fine. He didn't tell her not to worry, but there was such confidence and determination in whatever he said that she hung up each time, thinking it was a matter of hours before Bea Rose was found—not that the worst of her nightmarish worries would come true.

Soon she was arguing with him to come back. "Jonathon, you haven't slept at all. You're still driving around! You can't do much good running off into a ditch. I appreciate everything you're doing but—"

"Leah, I just thought of another spot I took her to... Got to go. Yeah, I'll quit in a while."

No, you won't, she thought when the line clicked. He cared and he wouldn't quit. He cared about a child who wasn't his and a woman who wasn't his, either.

In a relatively short time, and inadvertently, she had learned some startling information about Jonathon Jericho Wardwell. His tentative statement, "I think I love you," echoed in the now-quiet house. It was difficult for him to air emotions but easy to show them directly and physically. He was a man who did, not talked, and he cared.

When the phone rang this time, Leah knew, without knowing how, it was Jonathon.

"I've got her. She's okay. We'll be home in an hour."

"Jonathon...Jonathon..." Leah repeated brokenly until she figured out that the line was dead. Slumping down on the couch, she exploded with the stored anxiety, sobbing and sneezing and wailing incoherent words.

The bright afternoon sun was streaming in. The cats peeked suspiciously at her over the rim of their box and snuggled down again. Leah struggled to her feet, blowing her nose, and went off to shower quickly, putting on her long cotton caftan and slippers. Her feet burned from covering useless miles on the hardwood floors.

Fatigue, pain, everything was forgotten as soon as the familiar roar of Jonathon's truck filled the air. By the time Leah hit the front door, they were on the porch—a hollow-eyed man supporting a woebegone Beatrice Rose, wrinkled, wet and slightly green under her fresh coat of tan.

Leah sunk to her knees, clutching Bea and ignoring a rank smell rising off her. "Oh, honey...Bea, where in the world..." The words poured out too fast, running into each other and falling away in a babble of happiness.

Last night, her solemn oath was to hit first and hug later, but no anger came through the sheer joy of seeing them safe. *Them*, she confirmed by looking up at Jonathon through moist eyes. She cared, too.

"Got any coffee?" Jonathon asked, skirting them and walking in. "Never mind, I'll get it myself."

Leah took Bea's face between her hands and stared into her daughter's wide, round, glassy eyes. "Why?" she demanded. "Where and why?"

"Not now," suggested Jonathon very softly. "Let's sort out the whys and wherefores when we're thinking straighter...all of us."

Leah straightened up and kept a firm hand on Bea. "I'm going to put you in a warm, dry bed and you can sleep around the clock. But we will talk, Bea. A very serious, heavy talk, if you follow my drift."

"I really screwed up" came the barely audible whisper.

"Crudely put, but accurate in the extreme," muttered Leah, pushing her dirty and disheveled child ahead of her. She felt the tiny frame, the protruding shoulder blades and rubbed the lank strings of Bea's hair with affection. "Come on, I'll hold you up in the shower so you don't fall asleep and slip down the drain with the soap."

Bea hesitated and turned her head toward Jonathon. "I won't get a boat, will I? Not even if I earn the money. Not if I'm good the rest of the summer."

"Tomorrow," said Jonathon. He scratched the bridge of his nose and shrugged. "I don't know about the boat. This is not a particularly great moment to discuss it or for me to make a decision. We'll see."

"Okay," said Beatrice Rose in a very small voice. She made her foot-dragging way upstairs.

Leah leaned over the banister. "From the look of you, I recommend a hot shower right after hers. And I'll make up the guest room, Jonathon. You aren't going to take many more steps yourself."

His halfhearted refusal turned into a nod of assent. "I'll be right up. But I only want to sleep four or five hours, so set an alarm for me. I've got some errands that won't wait."

While Leah helped and hustled Bea through a fast wash and rinse, there was little conversation. Her drooping daughter was as subdued and close to tears as Leah had seen her in quite a while. Meekly, she submitted to having her head toweled dry and allowed Leah to escort her to bed.

Gnawing the inside of her lip, Leah sat on the edge of the bed and smoothed back Bea's bangs. Her child blinked up at the ceiling, one tear escaping to trickle back into her hair. Leah ached to know everything and understand it all, but there were moments to wait, not to press, and this felt like one.

"Am I going to be punished?" Bea's chin trembled.

Save the lecture and don't invoke the death penalty, something warned Leah. "Depends on what you mean by punishment," Leah said aloud. "You're feeling pretty awful right now and hurting; that's punishment. You made a big mistake and it affected a bunch of people, from Miranda Murching to some others whose names I didn't know before tonight... last night, I mean. You're going to have to take the responsibility for scaring us, putting unnecessary work and worry on others. But mistakes can usually be corrected and made right, as long as no one got hurt."

"I hurt you," Bea said, barely audibly. "I'm sorry."

Leah was so overwhelmed for a minute that she bit deep on the inside of her cheek. "Wow," she said finally and in all sincerity. "Beatrice Rose, this running away was bad. It was the pits, frankly. But I believe you just grew up, seeing me as a real person and not only as Mom, and by apologizing, not excusing."

She drew the covers up and kissed the slight, still figure several times before getting off the bed. The lowered shades did not block all the light from the room; there was a pale glow, gold and warm, gilding everything with a tranquil beauty.

When Leah reached the door, Bea spoke up, her voice blurred with approaching sleep. "I wasn't running away.

Honest. I had to get away—for a while—to think. I wasn't sure whether I liked or hated it here. I don't want it to matter, one way or the other. It's a dopey town...but it matters. Jonathon's neat and Bethany Peacham...and the cats..."

"It matters," Leah repeated softly in the hallway. She rested her forehead on the carved woodwork, feeling drained and empty. With the danger over, she should have expected more peace or exhilaration. With Beatrice Rose dropping her slick, savvy facade, she should be more pleased.

But something was missing. Leah massaged the ache in her neck, unable to pinpoint the source of the discontent, and decided she was hungry. After she made up the guest room, she'd fix a feast more sumptuous than black coffee and aspirin.

The sheets were turned back, the pillows fluffed, and Leah was cursing the intricacies of the digital clock she was trying to set when Jonathon appeared. He was clad in two bath towels, one draped around his neck and one precariously slung around his hips. He looked good in terry cloth—too good to look at for too long. Her language improved immediately, but so did her circulation.

Jonathon did not seem perturbed. He buffed his arms and chest before running his fingers like a rake through his sleek, wet hair. "Got things all squared away with Bea?"

"Not quite," Leah said, watching the towel's angle become acute. "She claims she didn't run away. We couldn't make much headway after that because her eyelids slammed shut."

"It could be true. She was stranded at the old Mark Light, ten miles north. The lighthouse was closed down in '48, boarded up. I took her there to show it to her one day.

I used to play pirate and light keeper, hide from my little sister at Mark Light.''

She didn't know he had a sister. She didn't know very much about him at all, and the bedroom had grown very small and crowded. Jonathon was blocking the door, whether he was aware of it or not.

"The lighthouse is stuck at the end of a narrow, rocky spit," he was saying. "After the storm hit, the wind kicked breakers all over the path back. She stayed put, rather than get washed away. I hope it scared the strut out of her but didn't break her spirit."

"That's a nice way of putting it," said Leah quietly. "I'll close the curtains and let you alone."

"Leah," he said in a funny, harsh voice, "don't . . ."

She paused, her fingers clinging to the drapery cords, her face and throat flushed, hearing a different note, feeling a heat stronger than the summer sun outside.

"Don't what?" she asked, struggling against a sudden giddiness. "Don't close the curtains . . . or don't let you alone?"

The room was silent. Leah could see the houses of Fairharbor set below hers, the roofs shimmering, and the sea wrinkling and moving in the distance. Her aching had returned, sharper and deeper, and centered itself in her chest. She realized she was holding her breath, afraid to turn to him, afraid to break the silence.

"Don't stand in front of the light like that," he whispered. "You're not wearing—"

"Neither are you," she said, not letting him finish.

Leah wasn't sure what happened next or who moved first.

One minute she was watching specks of dust dance in the slanted beams of light. The next they were clinging together, locked in the swaying dance of lovers. Her arms held Jonathon as tightly as he held her, her mouth was as greedy and hard on his.

They could not get close enough, kiss deeply enough, although their bodies strained and shifted in tiny restless movements. His hands shaped her to himself wildly, drifting up and down, along her sides and hips, reaching around to stroke her thighs, unable to stop the random, ceaseless caresses.

The gentle, reluctant Jonathon was gone. She held a man whose mouth demanded, not asked, whose bold fingers knew he was exciting her and searched to stroke more fire, more heat into her. The caftan's fabric was bunched, pulled upward, and her robe was stripped off and discarded without a word. There was scant pause in the rough pressure of his kiss, the rhythmic thrust of his tongue.

"Leah, darling. Leah, love...I want you," he groaned in the tiny interval.

Then she felt his flesh on hers as he pulled her back into his warmth for the meeting of their bodies without barriers. The towel was gone and any thought of restraint with it. He pushed his hips against her, slowly, until she returned the motion, acknowledging the pleasure of feeling his arousal. Her soft sob of desire, mingled with anticipation, did not satisfy him long; his hand found hers, drew it down from his neck to slide it between their bodies until she held him.

Just touching him made her tremble, sway gently with the force of that hot, dark storm of need she'd denied so long. It was not the hard, urgent message of his body that shocked her but the quick, rippling flow of her own readiness. Like a sudden, unexpected squall that broke without warning, her hunger shook her.

"Make love to me, Jonathon," she said. "Now. Right now. It will happen, you said. It should happen."

"Leah, I don't..." There was less certainty in his hoarse voice than she expected.

Her blood was roaring like the sea gone mad, and her heart thundered, drowning out his words. "You want me. I want you, too. With me. In me."

His body answered for him. His fingers moved over her in long, passionate strokes until her thighs parted in readiness, eager for his touch, lighter, more tantalizing motions. Leah's eyes dilated, her hips began to rock gently, as the wide, wild darkness rolled and built in her.

"I imagined kissing you...tasting you all over," Jonathon said hoarsely, "but I don't think I dare. I'm too excited. And I want to give you what you want, whatever you want."

Blindly, Leah took a step backward. Another and another. He moved with her, their bodies never losing contact. Their faces were held firmly toward each other, their eyes speaking of hunger and need. She felt the edge of the narrow bed at the back of her legs and then the coolness of the sheets. She saw only Jonathon, almost lost in the glare and brilliance of sunshine.

She drew him down, welcoming his weight, the heated slide of his body over hers.

Hearing his harsh and labored breath excited her. Feeling the taut lines of his body quiver with barely restrained madness made her wilder, bolder. She knew he was struggling for control and to wait, but there was no need to wait. She, always slow to rouse and slow to satisfy before, was caught in the tide of a strange new frenzy.

"Don't stop," she was pleading, her lips tight against his ear. "Don't stop, please."

Her request made him shudder and tore a cry from deep in his throat, low and full. "No, I won't...I can't," Jonathon moaned, as she arched, opening herself to him.

With the force of a wave curling to dash itself on the beach, he lifted slightly, found her and thrust forward. She had to move, filled with such sudden power; she called to him, bursting with a storm that was howling to break, stabbed with lightning flashing and twisting. She had to follow the tide of his hips, rising and falling.

He went rigid, tensing his muscles, as if he could prolong this union and hold back the sea. Leah found the ebb and flow too strong to stop. She pressed up and circled her hips.

"Jonathon, I never wanted anyone so much— never...never..."

Admitting the truth and saying it aloud tore open the heaviness of emotion within her, releasing a flood of sensations. Jonathon's face above her lowered, softer and sweeter, while his body resumed the steady advance and retreat that made them one.

He wanted to give and she wanted to take, holding him, gripping him as tightly as she could. It was a little frightening to feel so intimately bound, but something other than fear, more compelling than caution, took Leah over. She gave herself up to the waves of pleasure breaking in her, and to Jonathon.

He was the sea cresting on the yielding sands. He was the surf pounding onto the shore, lifting her with him, taking her in the most complete and shattering possession she had known. Even when he was swept over the brink of his own ecstasy, she soared on for a while, feeling the storm of release die very slowly, shaking her with brief spasms.

Jonathon held her close for what seemed a long time. Then he slid and turned, cradling her with tenderness, watching her quietly. Leah saw the exhaustion etched deeply in his face and began to ease away from him. They could choose a better time to talk, though they had not been able to postpone making love.

"Wait a minute," he said hoarsely. His eyes were clouded and his voice thick with sleep. "There are things I should say, explain to you. I didn't mean to lose control, Leah. I hadn't ever gotten that crazy...but, God, you were so wonderful, so beautifully responsive..."

"Go to sleep," she whispered, putting her hand to his lips. "You're babbling. I don't want any analysis or an apology. I want you to sleep."

He groaned once and his eyes closed.

Five

Leah wondered briefly at Jonathon's absence on Sunday; he wasn't one to miss dinner. Monday, she assumed he had catching up to do. She did, certainly.

Struck by inspiration, she spent most of the morning composing ads for the local paper. Her earlier leads to craftsmen had been obtained by word of mouth but she had followed every one up and her well was running dry. Spreading the word in print might flush out a few more and it would be easier if they started coming to her.

A fully recovered Beatrice peeked over her shoulder and criticized the copy. "Sounds like you're opening a gift store in the house. Why don't you hit the big city exposure angle harder? 'Show your wares in Boston, New York...' Like that!"

"Thanks," said Leah dryly. "Why don't I outright lie and say, 'Come to me and I'll make you rich and famous'? Kate's gallery isn't in New York or Paris."

Bea squinted at the sketch Leah was doodling. "I like your diving porpoise, though."

"It's a whale, sounding."

"And you majored in fine arts?"

"Art history. I took a minor in ceramics," Leah shot back. "I'm a little rusty, maybe."

"Naval jelly," prescribed Beatrice. "Jonathon says it takes rust off like a dream. Is it okay if I go see if Miranda and I are still friends and stop by Jonathon's? I want to row, but I have to get his permission to take the skiff."

"I am sufficiently impressed," Leah said. "Asking permission all over the place, mending fences...did you feed the menagerie?"

"Uh-huh!" Bea was poised like a marathon runner, ready to bolt.

"Okay, honey." Leah gave Bea a kiss and the fish-eye to her ad design. "It is sort of Flipper-ish... Oh, and tell Jonathon I decided to have him make the bookcases, will you? We can take them back with us. They'd fit in our apartment, stacked near the radiator."

"We had beautiful bookcases in the old house," Bea reminisced wistfully. "The big oak ones with the glass doors and the millions of drawers and hidey-holes to play with..."

Leah shook her head and quit fattening up her dolphin into a whale. "Those bookcases were your father's... *are* his. Law books. If I had them, we'd have to live out in the hallway or sleep in them."

Bea chuckled and whipped out of the house, slamming the screen door only half as hard as usual. Leah chewed meditatively on the end of her pencil, wondering whether the transformation would hold. Even more important, was the change all for the good?

She detected a case of hero-worship in the making. It was natural for Bea to seek male approval, she supposed, and there were worse men to admire than Jonathon. But heroes had the troublesome tendency to turn out to be merely humans, crushing disappointments to ten-year-olds.

And to bigger girls, too, something perverse in Leah said. She must not expect too much or hope too much. Perfection in a man was a much younger and sillier girl's dream, no longer hers. Jonathon and she could enrich each other's lives without *being* each other's lives.

Sometimes the past still smarted when Leah considered how deeply she had longed to be the perfect wife, the perfect mother and how often she forgot about perfecting Leah, the person. Years ago, she had loved her pottery but she had consigned her skill and interest to the garage—along with her potter's wheel—and rarely thought about it since.

She thought about pottery, Jonathon and a million other unrelated subjects, while hanging over the *Anchor* editor's desk. Her copy was being meticulously checked by Mr. Windham when Charlie Cranberry brought up the subject, waiting his turn for consultation.

"I'm advertising, too," he said proudly. "I am into a new art form."

"What's that?" asked Leah cautiously. "You're abandoning your...what did you call it...'sacred plasticity of mud'?"

"Going into fossilized fuels and exploring the depths of the earth's soul," Cranberry exclaimed gleefully. He had the face of a zealot set loose.

Leah ventured a timid guess. "You are planning to carve lumps of coal or make constructions of cinders."

"Blueberry and I are buying the gas station on contract," he trilled. "I'm selling all my clay and equipment to smell gas fumes, feel grease on my hands, get in touch with the power of engines. I can sculpt a crumpled fender!"

"From one moribund business to another," said Mr. Windham curtly. "You see ten cars a week on Cove Road, you'll be seeing a mirage."

"Can I leave my copy with you?" Charlie asked anxiously. "I want to get back and run the lube rack a few more times."

"Sure, sure," said Mr. Windham. "Say hello to Clare for me, Charles."

"Blueberry. Cranberry," cried the fleeing ex-potter.

"Horseapples," Mr. Windham said succinctly. "Beg your pardon, Mrs. Mackey."

"I wonder if he's planning to wear coveralls with a cranberry sewn on the pocket, or a smock?" mused Leah. "Well, the art world hasn't suffered a crippling blow."

"I'll run you right next to Jonathon Jericho Wardwell's regular ad," the editor said with a sly undercurrent. He looked over the papers Charlie had thrust in his hand and back to Leah. "Or would you prefer to be paired with the Natural Glories Gas Station?"

"Any spot you choose will be fine." Leah smiled. "You haven't seen Jonathon today, by any chance?"

Mr. Windham swiveled in his chair and rocked back, as if she was quizzing him on a truly difficult subject, but there was a gleam in his eye. That hint of humor and mischief was very familiar to Leah. The editor's blue eyes reminded her of an older version of Jonathon.

Windham. She put the family connection together while she was writing out the check for her ad. *Josiah Windham Wardwell.*

"No, I guess I haven't seen him," the old man finally announced. "I've made it around to all my usual news-gathering sources and he wasn't at any of them. Could have gone fishing with his dad, y'know. He'll do that. Get a dry spell in his schedule and take off to help Joe with his lobster pots."

Leah had observed the proper technique for prying in the past couple of weeks. She didn't ask anything directly or exclaim that she didn't know. She wagged her head sagely and kept her mouth shut. A long pause no longer meant the end of a conversation to her; she allowed Mr. Windham to reflect on what he'd said and acted as if there wasn't a thing she had to do, any other places to go.

"Course, he could be taking a break to finish one of his ships. When Jonathon gets right to the end of the project, he'll be eager as a boy to complete it."

"Of course," she murmured. "That's probably it. He was doing the *Lightning* clipper."

"She won't put a patch on the *Mayflower* he made me," proclaimed Mr. Windham. "Now hold on. I'll fetch the issue where I had pictures of my sixtieth birthday party and you'll see." He started to get up and sunk down again. "Naw, you go round to my place someday and get Martha to show you. A photograph doesn't do his handiwork justice. Best present anyone ever gave me."

"*Gave* you?" The words slipped out. Leah regained lost ground by slouching comfortably against the old man's desk and becoming engrossed in the yellow clippings fluttering above it.

"Those Wardwells were a tightfisted, uppity bunch," Mr. Windham went on affably. "They gave themselves airs, but it was the Windhams who were landed here first. That's why the *Mayflower* was a real fine gesture, I

thought. About time his side acknowledged where the
class was in our family tree.''

"Pilgrim stock," said Leah with a touch of fervor,
rooting the editor on. She was toying with the idea of
writing to a Boston acquaintance, a history scholar, and
asking her if inbreeding always resulted in mild battiness.
What century was Mr. Windham talking about? Did it
matter to him?

"Precisely," agreed the editor. He tipped back and
peered down his aquiline nose at Leah. "That isn't to say
that I don't respect their line, mind. Johnny-come-latelies
or not, the Wardwells did their bit. You've got a minute?"

It had already taken an hour to insert a two-by-three-
inch ad, discover Charlie Cranberry was in the vanguard
of Art, and catch the musty scent of New England family
history. Still, Leah calculated, patience might provide
clues as to what made the mysterious Jonathon Wardwell
tick and how she could wrangle a model ship. She could
always wait until she turned sixty and be given one, a truly
generous present, but she preferred a quicker approach.

Mr. Windham was rummaging through his file cabinets, slamming drawers and thumbing through back cop-
ies of the *Anchor*. This process also was drawn out; he
pulled several random issues to cluck over previous big
stories. Leah made polite expressions of interest about
such earthshaking events as the Peavys' roof being blown
away, the opening of the supermarket, and the contro-
versial removal of the sporting goods store's row of outside chairs for town ancients.

"Must have been a scandal," Leah said, feeling her
tongue lodge firmly in her cheek. "I can see, though, the
men didn't stand for it. Those same six chairs are filled

today." She only had to look across the street through his window to corroborate her statement.

He came shuffling back, flapping an issue. "Due in no small part to a splendid series of editorials, I modestly claim. Tradition! Right of assembly! The spirit of the law prevailed over the letter of the law, my dear woman. They were not obstructing traffic, not at all."

Leah took his paper, obediently scanning the page he indicated with his gnarled finger. Perhaps she should not be so amused or smug. Fairharbor's paper did not report an unending torrent of violence and ugliness or the constant, sickening supply of depressing, discouraging lead stories she abhorred in Boston's news. A grease fire in a kitchen, someone's wedding and whose gallstones were removed was, thankfully, important enough to rate space rather than terrorism or kidnapping. Small joys and sorrows were newsworthy.

"One of my better 'Profiles' pieces," Windham said with pride. "It was six years ago. Seeing as you have a personal interest in Jonathon Jericho—and vice versa, I hear—you'd appreciate it."

The grainy black-and-white photo was of two men, arms around each other's shoulders. A caption wasn't necessary; Jonathon hadn't changed and his father was only a slightly shorter, stockier but recognizable block from which he'd been chipped.

The profile was of the Wardwells en masse, and didn't focus primarily on Jonathon. Leah was disappointed, but she gleaned some fascinating tidbits from Mr. Windham's rather archaic style of writing. Shipbuilding was mentioned, but the grandfather's exploits as a booze smuggler during Prohibition were more prominently featured, giving her a chuckle.

"Shame! Shame!" she joshed. "I must ask Jonathon why he hasn't modeled the—" she skimmed the columns "—the *Liberty Belle*? What a fine name for a smuggler's ship!"

"Daniel Wardwell was an accomplished crook," complimented Mr. Windham with respect. "Never once got caught. Rum from the south, whiskey from Canada, beer made in his own basement. Helluva man and a sailor!"

Another line caught her eye and practically jumped off the page at her. Leah coughed, swallowing the wrong way. "Harvard? Jonathon Jericho went to Harvard?"

Mr. Windham bobbed his head and rocked back and forth on his heels. "He didn't have the bent for lobstering like his dad and there were some hard feelings, I can tell you. Joe wanted that father-son continuity more than anything else."

"Harvard?" gasped Leah. "He graduated from Harvard?"

"What ails you, woman? Are you a stammerer or an illiterate? My prose is factual and clear. Repeating is an odious habit."

"Forgive me," she said, "but he simply forgot to mention this minor fact, and I was surprised. I find a good many things around Fairharbor curious."

"Yes, I expect so," Mr. Windham said sympathetically. He eased his precious paper out of her fingers, refolding it neatly. "Well, you seem to be well thought of, despite being from outside and your irritating parroting. Where in Maine were you born? What did you say your maiden name was?"

"I didn't say." Leah edged for the door. "When you're ready to write a 'Profile' on me, I'll be happy to bend your ear."

He waved her goodbye. "Oh, that's okay. I was going to fill out my piece on your daughter's wandering off and Ray Coodey's splendid marshaling of his force. Watch for Friday's edition!"

"Wouldn't miss it," Leah groaned. Celebrity status was achievable in Fairharbor but not necessarily desirable. She envisioned Beatrice Rose buying up stacks of *Anchor*s to send to her friends and relatives. Anyone in town who didn't yet know about the incident would by Friday.

By the end of the week, Jonathon was a household staple who had become a scarce commodity. He had not called or dropped by. Leah could have accepted a complete report on his daily doings and state of health from Bea at dinner but secondhand information and his continuing absence were beginning to nettle her. Friday, she concluded her wheeling and dealing with a sweet octogenarian who cut sharper bargains than most scalpels and left the kittens leaping in and out of his beautifully carved cradle sample. Bea was too busy clipping the review of her recent adventure from the paper to walk to town, even to buy a scrapbook. It was a simple shopping trip, Leah assured herself, not a pursuit of the elusive Mr. Wardwell.

However, she found it necessary to stop in the doughnut shop, stroll by the lumberyard and go to the hardware store. Mr. Windham's favorite hotbeds of news and activity fell short of her expectations until she sighted Jonathon, pawing through bins somewhere among the vise grips and needle nose pliers.

"Excuse me," she said sweetly, tapping him on the back. "I'm looking for a left-handed widget bolt . . . and a friend. Have you seen either of them?"

Jonathon became flushed, coloring on his throat and cheeks, but he turned to face her. "Hi, Leah. I was planning to stop by this afternoon. Next week is the box supper, the dinner auction. I've been making a new buffet table and benches for the church."

"I heard rumors you went to a Harvard class re-union," hissed Leah when she saw several other patrons taking an interest in them.

Jonathon stiffened a bit before he laughed. "No, I don't go to those affairs. Never did! About the social on Friday—"

"Speaking of affairs," interrupted Leah, "you don't have to slink around, Jonathon, to avoid me. If it doesn't work for you, it doesn't. It doesn't have to be total rejection of our friendship, however. That's all I wanted to say."

"Oh, Lord, what a stupid thing to say..." He slapped his forehead and tossed the items he was holding back into the bin. "Leah, I was afraid to..."

"Stupid!" she trounced hard on his toe, forgetting he was wearing heavy boots and she had on sneakers. Mr. Windham's criticism of her repetitions occurred to her. "What did you think I'd think when you suddenly vanished for a week? You see Bea nearly every day but not me... Well, you are definitely..."

"Avoiding you," he said, taking her arm and trying to steer her behind the large pyramids of paint cans. "Yes, yes, I have been avoiding you. Hi, Mrs. Bellini!"

Leah resisted his strength for as long as she could but, short of decking him with a handy tool, there wasn't much to do but move. "Aha, you admit it. Do tell," she mocked.

"I can't stay away from you," he said. "I gave it my best shot this week and didn't do very well. You didn't see me but I saw you. I drove by every night, I watched you work in the yard Wednesday, and I know you went to the drugstore yesterday.'' He smiled, clearly embarrassed by his confession of spying.

"I finally found something that works on my allergy. I've tried every pill in stock and begged the pharmacist to order me a case. It's so great, this stuff, I may buy myself a fur coat for Christmas and be able to wear it."

"Aren't you going to make fun of me?" Jonathon asked. "My behavior? From Bea's talk of your life in Boston, I gather you're acquainted with smoother, more sophisticated types."

"True, no one quite like you," Leah replied. She lowered her voice. "They tend to be more impressed with themselves than I am. I told you I wasn't involved with anyone, Jonathon, and until very recently, I wasn't."

"Are you going to let me explain," complained Jonathon, "or do I have to write you a letter? I was wrong not to call. All right, I'm wrong and dumb and silly, but I had a problem."

"What's the problem? You or me?"

"Us," he whispered back, cupping his hand over her mouth to keep her quiet. "There's something I should have said the other night and I didn't. It's been bothering me since then, but I wasn't sure how to broach the subject. I let my great opportunity slip by me. I got shy, I guess."

Leah made choked noises into his hand until he took it away and repeated herself more intelligibly. "Shy? I didn't notice. Oh, damn, I did it again!"

"Did what again?"

"Now you're doing it. Never mind. Go ahead, Jonathon."

"Full steam ahead," he said, drawing a deep breath and peering all around. "Leah, first of all, I'm wildly in love with you."

She stepped back and looked up at him from under her eyebrows. When had she left Massachusetts and moved to this state of confusion? Nothing seemed to make sense anymore or to follow a predictable course. Bea ran off to contemplate the danger of being happy. Jonathon stayed away because he was in love with her and they had shared a wonderful, intimate experience.

"I'm doing fine, Mr. Olson. I found the picture hooks and wire," she said weakly to the store owner as he passed. "Jonathon, please speak slowly if you intend to continue. I'm an outsider. I don't follow the native customs and speech as fully as I imagined I did."

He smiled, his eyes lit with delight. "You will understand because you just made the exact point I was about to. I'm not like the men you're used to and I didn't plan on making lo... what happened. I set out to establish a strong foundation for us to build on and grow together. Now I can't act as though it didn't happen or I didn't want it to."

"Heaven help me," breathed Leah. "I am almost following this astounding logic. In case you were in doubt, I didn't expect or plan... you know what."

Someone bumped into her, pushing Leah flush into Jonathon. He steadied her but took his hands away quickly and let them drop; they hung at his sides as if he wasn't sure what to do with them.

Usually Olson's did a slow, steady business, but the local interest in redecorating had become inexplicably brisk. Male traffic to and from wall enamels was threatening to clog the narrow aisle. Jonathon stalked over to the leaf rakes and snow shovels at the back wall and urged Leah to follow. She reluctantly complied, loudly registering her preference for a less public setting.

"Not until I manage to say what I have to," Jonathon insisted. "That's why I didn't have the nerve to come up to the house. I wasn't sure I'd go through with it and not get—" he was peeking over the shelves to make sure no one was crouched behind the sacks and boxes "—carried away or out of control."

"This is ridiculous!" muttered Leah. "Are we being chaperoned by the rest of clientele? Is that it?"

He became solemn, almost grave. "Exactly, Leah. I don't take love lightly. To me, you aren't a happy accident bumping into my life. I have to know what you intend for us. I've waited years to meet you, love you. At least, that's not what I want...a casual fling, a temporary interlude."

She began glancing furtively around. "You want to know if my intentions are *honorable*? Okay! We met less than a month ago, Jonathon, but I care about you. I missed you this week."

His medium blue eyes bored into her, not blinking, not leaving hers for a fraction of a second. The same mouth that had brought her completely back to life was tense and thin. He folded his arms across his chest and gave his head a very small but telling shake.

"You evade," he said. "I avoid. But no more! I'd tell you if I only wanted a couple of months and was able to wave a lighthearted goodbye when you sail away. That isn't the truth, though. I can't...and I won't."

Similar sentiments had come from her very mouth, her very soul two years ago. But then, she was Michael's accuser, demanding an end to white lies and half-truths and telling him she could not—would not—live comfortably with him any longer. In the midst of luxury, Leah had sworn she couldn't be untrue to herself and live a lie.

At the rear of a hardware store, she was feeling pinned to the wall.

"What are you doing?" she wailed, spreading her hands wide in dismay. "What are you asking me for, Jonathon? You scolded me for being in such a hurry. Well, maybe I am—with some things. But I can't make any commitments I'm not entirely sure I should. I won't be rushed to say words or make promises I can't keep!"

"There," he said softly. "There's the truth, or most of it. I was asking for that. What I'm doing is proposing to you. I don't happen to have a ring at the ready but I could find a suitably sized washer to tide us over. Will you marry me?"

"No!" She was torn between laughter and tears. "Did you hear what I said?"

"Yes. Did I come through loud and clear? Just as long as we both know where we stand, I'm satisfied. I'll keep asking, by the way."

"This is totally insane," Leah said. "I don't think I'll get any argument on that statement."

"Not from me," Mr. Olson's voice interjected. Part of the rear paneling moved, and the storeroom door swung open. He took a few timid steps, excusing himself up, down and sideways as he tried to ease past them. "I do have invoices to do, y'know. I would have come out sooner, but I was expecting you'd move on any time. No, sir, I do not listen at keyholes as a rule. Couldn't hear much, either, rest assured. Well, uh, back to work."

Leah snorted, exasperated. Jonathon smiled.

"My honorable intentions will be widely known by dark," he said.

"We'll be featured in the *Anchor*, most likely," growled Leah more gruffly than she felt. The air was cleared, and it appeared that Jonathon meant what he said; he needed to make his position plain and her simple no sufficed.

"Give you a lift?" he offered. "I'd like to find out what you're planning to fix for next Friday's social. I'll pick you and Bea Rose up at five-thirty, regardless of your menu, but I won't bid on your box supper if you're whipping up some concoction with bean sprouts and mushrooms."

Her defense of an occasional meatless, weight-watching meal sprang out so fast that Leah nearly missed his invitation at the core of the kidding. They were on the road before she snapped to his assumption that she was going at all.

"Bea will go," she said. "She's into one of her ravenous phases, one meal taken continuously. But, Jonathon, I'm not. It's strictly a townies' gathering, organized more to trade digs at each other's cooking than recipes or to raise money for community projects. Frankly I'm a coward. All those women would have a field day with my peach cobbler recipe and my recent parental incompetence."

"What's wrong with your peach cobbler?" he asked in mock horror.

"I put raisins in it. Always have. My grandmother taught me that way, and I feel guilty if I leave them out."

Jonathon braked but left the engine running in front of Chandler House. "And what sin of parenting, pray tell, are you guilty of?"

Leah made her voice strain for the high tones of cattiness reached in Miranda's post office. "Oh, my, raisins in her cobbler and raising kids is quite beyond that woman, too. Why, her child ran away. No discipline, no common sense."

Jonathon laughed but it was short and without much humor in the sound. "You pinpointed the worst in us, Leah, the pettiness. Although there's bigness of spirit, even greatness here. Anyone who has kids understands they get as much grief as gravy and that there's no best recipe. The others or the overly righteous? Hey, they don't know saltwater from cider, so who cares?"

"Well-l-l," she drawled, stalling for a minute. "All right, why not?"

A night off without a trauma was overdue and any gathering could be fun, with the right attitude. She might stumble on some undiscovered, reclusive artist who swooped down from the bluffs to gorge at the celebration of local culinary talent.

"Five-thirty," said Jonathon, reaching across her to open the door.

The contact they made was slight, but it reminded Leah that not every issue had been completely aired in the hardware store. Perhaps Jonathon knew where they stood; she was not as sure. She scratched at a mosquito bite, but the real itch was to ask him a few pointed, somewhat indelicate questions.

She smiled at him, making no effort to slide out. "Let me get this straight. You proposed. I declined. But we're going to see each other Friday. A date, I suppose?"

"Somewhat more than that," Jonathon said, with a perplexed expression. "I figured you understood. I'm courting you, all open and proper. And you'll see me tomorrow when I bring your bookcases around . . . They're finished."

"I understand I'm experiencing culture shock," sighed Leah, clutching her bag of doughnuts and hardware store purchases. "Is courting another euphemism? I believe that expression went out with the bustle and high-button shoes. I get the distinct impression you are sorry that what happened, happened. I didn't have any regrets, Jonathon."

He shifted uneasily behind the steering wheel, staring out the windshield. "I don't want you to be sorry. I want you to be mine. And I'd like to hear you say it before we make love, not when we're driving each other crazy, incapable of thinking beyond the next second, the next kiss."

"Are you saying... we're not going to...?" Leah forgot about being delicate in her amazement. "Good grief, is sex abnormal, unheard of or improper here? I don't know if it matters to you or not, Jonathon, but I hadn't slept with anyone in almost three years. Not until last week, anyway. You're acting as if I might be the type of woman who put notches on her belt for every affair. You aren't just another man!"

The speed with which he moved was frightening, catching her off guard. Jonathon turned, grabbed and held her immobile. His eyes were troubled, and when he spoke, it was with a gravelly, hard voice.

"I'll be real blunt, Leah. If I wanted any woman, there are plenty of women around. If I wanted sex, there's plenty for the asking. I haven't been at sea or celibate for years. I know I acted like I had the other night and I am sorry about that! No woman before ever excited me like you do... I've never let my body rule my brain before."

He brought his face very close to hers. The heat of his breath caressed her face, but his hands were stiff and rigid on her, not particularly loving. "Not just another man, no," he said, in a gritty whisper. "I don't want to be anything but your only man. Before the summer ends, I intend to be."

His fierceness was a facet of his personality she'd never seen, a hard gleam in his blue eyes, a sharp edge in a man who appeared easygoing to a fault. He was as rough cut as the granite cliffs right now, as unyielding and tough as any of his ancestors.

All the uncertainties of life, the doubts and disappointments in love that Leah felt didn't seem to mean anything to him. She felt herself tense, more a prisoner of her memories than a captive in his arms. There was no "only," anymore. No "forever," no permanence in a world of disposable everything—from silverware to people.

"I've got to go," she said thickly. "You better let me get busy or I'll be out of a job before the month is up, never mind September."

"Sorry." Jonathon frowned, releasing her quickly. "I didn't mean to scare you. You see, I almost got carried away again."

"I'm not scared of you," Leah insisted as she got out, hoping her sincerity matched his. "I get afraid for other people, not myself, lately."

But as she walked slowly to the house, she wondered. How fair was Fairharbor? How safe was this place if she was inevitably going to hurt Jonathon or be hurt once more?

Six

No opera opening was better attended than the box-supper auction, the highlight of Fairharbor's summer social scene. Leah and Beatrice Rose gawked at the sight of their first hint of a parking problem, the trucks and cars of outlying neighbors inching through the main thoroughfare. Jonathon blew the horn constantly but it was in greeting, not admonition. People honked back, waved, shouted greetings with the same high spirits usually reserved for football games and family reunions.

"Look, they set benches and tables outside the hall!" Beatrice blasted in Leah's ear. She was wedged in the middle but unhampered, smothering Leah as she leaned over to hang out the window. "And they put miniature lights in the trees. It looks like a Parisian café, doesn't it?"

"Not quite," Leah retorted, shoving her daughter back in place with her dinner basket. "Very pretty, though. Oh, Bea, hang in there! You nearly ripped the cat's head off."

The damage was not as gruesome as it sounded. Leah had followed Miranda's, Jonathon's *and* Bea's instructions to the letter preparing her offering for the festivities. Each lady was expected to deliver her supper packaged as creatively, attractively and uniquely as possible.

Leah's preference for a brown paper bag with a ribbon tied around it was immediately nixed by Jonathon. She fancied she had more than risen to the occasion with her calico cat, stuffed paws and tail sewn onto a willow basket and complete with embroidered jaunty smile and straw whiskers. Both ears drooped and its close-set button eyes gave her creature a rather evil aspect, but Leah was supremely pleased, more protective of her creation than of any of the live kittens running rampant in her house.

"You should be flattered, Mom," Beatrice chided, darting ahead to catch up with a friend. "At least Jonathon will bid on your basket, Sphinx and all. What if no one wanted it?"

"What are you going to eat?" Leah hollered in the approximate direction Bea had vanished. "Beatrice Rose Mackey!"

"Let her go," said Jonathon. "Kids generally wander from person to person at this thing, eat everything there is to sample and end up sick for two days."

"You folks really know how to have fun," Leah sighed. "Oh, good grief, look at those boxes and baskets. Kate Chandler would go ape and buy them for a window display! They're ... gorgeous." She gave her cat a consoling pat and one of its eyes detached, the button rolling into the crowd.

"Put it up there," instructed Jonathon. "Don't make a face, Leah. It looks better, honestly. Like it's winking."

"I could pull the other eye off," she laughed. "Then, it wouldn't have to see the competition."

She moved off toward the cluster of women tagging and arranging the huge array of dinners in the front of the hall. Fairharbor boasted a town hall, a community center and three churches; residents rarely mentioned that one building served for all these bodies.

"Oh, that's cute, Mrs. Mackey," an eager volunteer cried, snatching Kitty Klaws from Leah. "Sarah Jane, see the nice dog she made. And he's winking, too."

Leah lost interest in setting the record straight. Behind the banquet table display, there was a series of glass cases with town treasures, trophies and memorabilia stored. She wove her way in and out of people, maneuvered around the long tables and steered directly for the model ship she spotted.

Unmistakably, it was one of Jonathon's. The small engraved brass plate at the base confirmed her opinion and also drove her into another fit of envy and bewilderment. "Gift of J. J. Wardwell," the plaque began, nearly finishing Leah off. Mr. Windham had a gift. Fairharbor had a gift. But she couldn't buy one!

"Tell me you're not weird," she said to Jonathon, somewhat breathlessly. The trip back to him had taken ten minutes, fighting the crowds surging to survey the night's items before the bidding.

"Okay," he answered amiably, "I'm not weird. What am I?"

"A philanthropist or economically slow," guessed Leah. "Do you know—I mean, *really* know—what you could sell a ship like *Sea Witch* for? But you! You gave her to the town."

"I remember," he said mildly. "What number is your Feline Feast? I may faint from hunger."

"Two digits," Leah barked, "not four digits, as in the price of a fine ship. Eighty-one."

He shot her a reproving look as Oscar Peavy, the mayor, started warming up the crowd with his salty jokes and shaggy-dog stories. "I charge for work, not for my play, hobby and therapy. Making things to order is what I do for a living. As far as my models go, I do what I like and when I like."

The bidding began with a giant papier-mâché lobster, a brilliant scarlet production filled with enough food to feed a small army. Oscar was in his glory, fondling the beast, wiggling its pipe cleaner antennas and driving the price as high as he possibly could.

"I told you I used to be a potter," argued Leah. "I loved every perfect piece I turned out and wanted to keep them all. Pretty soon, I was living in a studio apartment with six teapots and matching cups, three complete sets of dishes, more pitchers than the National League and cartons of mugs under my bed. I didn't need the money and I didn't particularly want to sell but, boy, it was a thrill when I had to. And people bought and used *my* ceramics."

"That was you. This is me," said Jonathon bluntly. "I finish two a year, if I'm lucky. They aren't hanging from the rafters, you may have noticed."

"Thirty-seven." Oscar guffawed. "A large crock filled with vegetarian delicacies and a certificate for five gallons of gas. Feeds three. No, the meal will not give you gas, Elmer. That wasn't what I said."

"Charlie and Clare's contribution," whispered Leah. "He's selling out and joining the establishment, in a sense. I hope he didn't fry anything in motor oil."

"You know," Jonathon said, glancing around the assembly, "if you wanted to show your heart was in the right place, you'd find out what Charlie would take for his potting equipment and become a local artisan."

"What are you talking about? As if I don't have enough to do." Leah shot him a quizzical look. "I'm on the buying end, not the selling end."

"Well, it's just a thought and probably an idle one, but there might not be as much resistance to you as an outsider, the city lady with the bucks, if you were actually producing."

"Ingratiate myself into the community? Make me one of the residents? I don't think so."

She tugged at his sleeve as her basket was hauled out and deposited on the lectern Oscar used as an auction block. The cat's head lolled drunkenly. Following, as it did, the three-foot lighthouse constructed of white-frosted sugar cookies, Leah's basket wouldn't fetch fifty cents, she mused.

"And here we have..." Mayor Peavy did a double take, reading the menu stapled to the handle. "Ah, Mrs. Mackey's shrimp rolls, peach cobbler and—if the buyer desires—a genuine kitten, pick of the litter. Not to consume, I hope."

A wail across the room indicated that Bea had heard. Leah covered her guilty face with one hand. She hadn't expected the bonus to be announced.

Jonathon leaned down and whispered in her ear. "You didn't stuff a kitten in that basket, did you? Shame on you."

"Not in the basket! But there's six of them leaping around, eating everything in sight, tipping over plants..."

"Three dollars," Jonathon sang out loudly.

Bea Rose rushed up, red-faced and with both hands full of food. "How could you, Mom? I adore them all!"

Some foolhardy soul bid four dollars and Jonathon had to go to five. "Don't worry," he said out of the corner of his mouth to Bea. "The little bugger is safe! I have seven dollars with me. We'll keep the pack of them."

"*You'll* keep the pack of them?" shrieked Leah. "They're climbing up *my* bedspread and drapes, not yours."

"I've got seventy-five cents with me," Bea said, digging frantically in her pockets. "It's all yours, Jonathon."

"It's the carpenter's cat for six-fifty!" announced Oscar with a wink. "Heave to, Mr. Wardwell, and pay up."

Jonathon went off to collect his bounty, and Leah attempted to forestall the argument she knew was coming.

"Now, Beatrice," she said, holding up her hand like a stop sign, "before you say a word you'll regret, think! We cannot have seven cats in our apartment. Our lease clearly indicates we can't have even one. Sooner or later, you have to face the fact that we are not in the flea circus business. You want to earn money for a boat? How about having a yard sale and include the kittens? You can keep the proceeds. We can't keep the cats."

Bea Rose stuck her lower lip out as far as it would go. "Maybe . . ." she allowed, grumpily. "Next time I talk to Dad, I'll see if he'll take one and give me visitation rights."

"Talk to Karen first," suggested Leah. "You stand a better chance with her as your ally. Michael thinks cats are sneaky, nasty animals."

Bea pondered this approach for a minute. "But . . . but he always said we didn't have any pets because you were allergic."

"That was very thoughtful of him, very considerate," Leah said as neutrally as possible. She didn't bother to mention that over the past two years Michael hadn't acquired any pets, either. Bea was bright; she'd make her own connections.

"The cobbler smells great," Jonathon said. He had staked out a corner bench in the hall, showing Bea where she could find them after the festivities died down. "I already decided I'll take the kitten with extra toes. His feet look like dinner plates, that one."

"I'd like to know how you stay so skinny and eat so much," Leah complained as they waded through bodies. "In fact, Jonathon, there are lots of things I'd like to know about you. Like why you never mentioned Harvard or what you got your degree in. It's usually a mark of prestige, not a badge of shame to hide."

"It was a long time ago, another life ago. Economics," he said tersely. "I didn't bring it up because you hired me to fix the house, not advise you about investments or stocks. Okay? Now let's enjoy ourselves . . . and eat."

It came out as an order more than a request. But Leah decided to let the subject drop. She had conceived a plan, watching Oscar Peavy at work and listening to his grandiose boasts for Fairharbor. The money raised tonight was intended to support a variety of programs and improvements for the town. She might not get enthused about a state-of-the-art fire engine for the volunteer force or steel litter baskets or new swings for the playground but the people around her had been spurred on, bidding higher.

Their dinner companions cooperated unwittingly with her. While Jonathon wolfed down her meal in record time, Leah chatted away amiably with them.

Miranda, happily, was one of the bench's occupants. Her tart commentary on the event's success couldn't have served Leah better if she'd written the script herself. "Seven hundred and eighty-nine dollars," sniffed Miranda disdainfully. "All this hoopla and folderol to raise that! And don't forget, they bought new bunting this year and Jonathon made some tables. Benches, too. We'll have a puny sum left after expenses. Oscar can buy a headlight for the fire engine and one teeter-totter for the park."

"I donated my table and benches," Jonathon corrected. He placed half the cobbler on a paper plate in front of him and then generously offered the others a taste.

"Mercy, what are those things in it?" asked Miranda.

"Not bugs," Leah said quickly. "Sultanas."

Someone down the table began to retell the story of how Samuel Tilton demolished a bench last year.

"... so Big Sammy bought three meals for himself, sat down right there, wasn't it, and bang! Down goes..."

Leah felt her courage and the chance slipping away. It was now or never.

"If you sold me a ship," Leah said nonchalantly to Jonathon, "I'd raffle it off back in Boston. Or, I think, Kate might consider taking bids for it and donating the sale price back to Fairharbor for good works. She'd get publicity, a tax deduction, and you'd get—"

"No," said Jonathon, without missing a bite. "Not for sale."

"Why not?" she persisted. "You gave the town a ship and your labor. You could have presented Peavy with a check from Kate for a couple of thousand dollars instead."

"I could have," Jonathon agreed, "but we would have canceled out this evening's value and everyone else's contribution to the town's future. Both of those things, the annual gathering and the general participation, are more important than my playing big-shot."

She took advantage of the loud burst of laughter over another box-supper reminiscence to argue. "You are so damned stubborn, Jonathon, and you're wasting a real gift, a talent. What you do with wood and string and patience is practically a lost art. Why not get the audience acclaim and money you deserve?"

"Because I do it for myself," he growled. "Don't you have something you do purely to please yourself? A private world you can go to for the sheer joy of doing it?"

"Frankly, no," Leah said angrily, with a touch of resentment. "I've been too busy making a living, making a home. Oh, I know what you're talking about. Relaxation, self-expression, and so on. That's how I got started puttering around in the ceramics studio in college."

"You should have stuck with it," he opined. "It isn't too late, though. You can always go back to potting, I suppose."

"You changed the subject," Leah said, exasperated. She stuffed the silverware and empty plates back into her basket. "I wasn't talking about me, but you. And a ship. And why you're averse to selling me one. Think community spirit!"

"Make me a coffee mug that holds more than two sips and I'll discuss it further," he challenged. "A cup that doesn't tip over, keeps the brew hot and has a handle I can put more than one finger in comfortably."

"That's stupid! What does that have to do with—"

"Those who can, do. Those who can't, lecture or try to wheedle the goods from those who can," Jonathon said in a theatrical aside.

"Shut up!" Leah tried to pinch his midsection but there wasn't any spare tire to grab on to. "It's been ten years, sure, since I centered a blob of clay but I could...if I wanted to."

He extracted his wallet and took out a dollar bill, folding and holding it up to his lips. *Put your money where your mouth is* came through loud and clear, although he didn't utter a peep.

"I was good," Leah said hotly. "Everyone who saw my work said it was very clean and original. I sold pieces! But it's very time-consuming, Jonathon, and I already have a job. Several, in fact. And it isn't simply buying a wheel and borrowing a shovel to dig a few buckets of clay out of a bank. I'd need drying shelves and a kiln..." She ran down an impressive list of essential items.

"I can build anything you need," he said evenly. "Cheap! You've got free days now and then. What with these ads you've taken out, people are stopping by to see you. Right? And there's evenings, weekends, national holidays and total eclipses of the moon and sun when nothing's happening."

"Oh, you," said Leah, disgustedly. Unfortunately, the idea was appealing and taking root. "Cranberry is a total flake. He'll want a preposterous sum for his crummy foot-driven equipment."

"Barter," Jonathon said, with a gentle nudge to her ribs. "Do your best city-slicker con job. Talk about the common bond you have in 'Ahhht' and the joys of freeing oneself from crass material considerations."

Leah was seized with a fit of giggles. Jonathon had his hand pressed dramatically to his chest, lips pursed, and an incredibly intense, eye-rolling expression.

"All right, I will," Leah gasped. "Just to satisfy my curiosity, not to do anything rash and foolish...or expensive!"

"Good, I'm going to suck around Mary Peacham and see if I can sweet-talk her out of a piece of pistachio torte.

She makes it every year for bake sales and birthdays, and I never get there fast enough to snap it up."

"Oh, you didn't like raisins in the cobbler," Leah accused his retreating back. "Not brave enough to say it to my face, eh?"

Jonathon whipped around with a Cheshire cat grin. "Loved it! Top drawer and the best! Mean it sincerely, babe. We must have lunch, so have your machine call my machine. I just have to give ol' Mary a warm and fuzzy feeling for the sake of auld lang syne. Catch you soon."

His phony, high-powered businessman routine was as good as his fragile art critic. Leah stood there, jaw lowered, and watched him duck and dive through the crowd. How funny and how weird! For a man who made such an effort to be plain and simple, Jonathon often gave hints that he was well acquainted with other life-styles, elaborate urban and sophisticated.

But he didn't talk about living anywhere else or doing anything for a living but carpentry. Leah couldn't dredge up a single fact or piece of evidence that bore out her suspicions. She'd have to ask him directly soon and hope he'd tell her. When Jonathon wanted a subject closed, it took a crowbar to pry him open. However, if he said something, it was true.

She elbowed her path over to Cranberry and Blueberry. While she warmed up the couple with polite and silly chatter, she was busy recalling how many years Jonathon had been in Fairharbor without leaving. Ten. He had said he hadn't left the immediate area for ten years.

Afterward, she regretted her preoccupation with Jonathon. Her purchase of the wheel and gear, glazes and a drying rack could be forgiven. Charlie Cranberry was incredibly happy to put his equipment into her hands for a reasonable price. He threw in free two fifty-gallon barrels of clay he'd personally, lovingly collected and cleaned, making a lengthy speech about the spirituality of this particular batch. However, Leah had recklessly agreed to take all his stock on hand. She was paying him by weight, not for merit, but she scuttled off, the new owner of the entire Cranberry Collection, debating how to best dispose of this treasure.

"I did something rash and foolish," she informed Jonathon. He was mashing the crumbs of Miss Peacham's pistachio torte with a fork, not willing to let one escape. "And I volunteered you and the truck to help me move my purchase."

Jonathon gave Mary Peacham a peck on the cheek and her fork back. "Swell. I'm not complaining."

"You will be," Leah said, "when you find out how many boxes of ugly stoneware you're about to tote. You'll wish you hadn't mentioned the wheel, let alone encouraged me."

"We'll see," said Jonathon, escorting her out. "You made a good deal, I gather."

"Unbelievable would be a fairer description," Leah said with a laugh. "I have to find out who has a kiln I can rent to use when I'm ready. Any more bright ideas?"

"I'll build one. I wasn't kidding."

"Oh, no! A kiln is a permanent structure and I don't have Kate's permission to put additions on her property."

He put two fingers in his mouth and whistled sharply, drawing Bea's attention to them. The notes were no more piercing than the look he gave Leah. "And, you also wish to remind me, you are taking on a project for the remaining weeks, not making a permanent change. Any permanent change is out."

"I didn't say that," Leah insisted. "You did. And we are talking about a ceramics oven, not our relationship. Are you picking a fight with me?"

He assumed a thoughtful posture. "Maybe. Fighting is one-on-one and gets the blood fired up. I'd prefer a different kind of interaction but if this is all we can do, it'll have to be our hot and heavy form of expression."

"If this is all we can do...I like that!" Leah pushed him aside, snatching her droop-eared cat basket back. "I'm not the one hiding behind the spray paint and glossy enamels in a hardware store, acting all gosh and golly and avoiding a handshake."

Jonathon held up his hand, signaling Bea's approach. "Calm yourself, Leah. We can fight later."

"This is not a fight!" she yelled. "I am simply explaining to you how your own old-fashioned code has placed severe limits on...on expression."

Jonathon seized the cat's stuffed tail and yanked it free, brandishing it at her. "I'm old-fashioned, meaning I value you and want love to stay a beautiful four-letter word and not a dirty one. I want it to last longer than an hour and mean more than two ships passing in the night."

"Oh, and I don't!" She pulled the cat tail back and whomped him solidly with it, sending a shower of white fibers into the air, snowing down on them. "Well, let me tell you, Mr. Wardwell, this is the twentieth century, not the one we'd choose, maybe, but the one we're stuck in. Love and marriage no longer go together like horse and carriage."

"This is great," Bea Rose piped. "What's it about?"

"Love," snarled Jonathon.

"Liberation," Leah countered.

"Everybody's watching," noted Bea. "Are you going to hit him again? I never saw you actually fight with anyone before."

"I'm not fighting!" Leah screamed. "Mature adults negotiate and compromise!"

Jonathon reached out and fluffed her hair, releasing a small cloud of polyester snowflakes. His lips twitched suspiciously, holding back laughter. "Absolutely," he agreed. "Modern people have risen above all the base, raw emotions—aggression, passion, jealousy, love..."

"Oh, I see!" Bea chirped brightly. "That's why Mom and Daddy never fought and they're so polite to each other. They're modern and they don't love each other anymore."

"A perceptive child," Jonathon said with a magnificent, triumphant smile.

"Whose life hangs by a slender thread," Leah finished. "Go wait outside, Beatrice, by the truck. We may have to walk home."

"Karen dumped a plate of canapes on Daddy at a party," her daughter confided. "He wouldn't help her serve and he was paying too much attention to some grossly obese and horribly important lawyer from Wilmington. And Daddy adores her."

Having delivered her pearl of wisdom, Bea walked away jauntily.

"Karen has just climbed a notch in my estimation," Leah said and began to grin, despite her best efforts to keep a straight face. "Once I wanted to lean across the table and set the *Times* on fire while Michael was engrossed in it. I should have. Might have caught his attention."

"Might still be married to him," suggested Jonathon.

Leah howled with laughter. "Then thank goodness I didn't. I didn't know what happy was until I stopped giving and going to those boring, stupid parties. There's more to life than making sure Michael had clean underwear and serving on the right committees to advance his career."

"This stuff itches," moaned Jonathon, scratching inside the collar of his shirt. "Can we go? I've gotta shake it out. Hey, I'll buy you guys an ice cream cone on the way. Peace offering?"

"Be still, my heart," Leah said, taking his arm. "I don't know if I can take such excitement. Double dip? Triple?"

"The sky's the limit," Jonathon retorted. "Go wild! Get sprinkles on top, if you want 'em. Nuts!"

"I'm beginning to think you are." Leah smiled, though. "We have resolved nothing, by the way."

"Sure we have," he contradicted. "Even your daughter has it figured out. You love me. You're fighting *it*, not me. I just have to make sure you don't love me when you're holding a heavy, blunt instrument—at least for a while."

She pursed her lips and made a huge, resounding raspberry. "There is my mature and modern opinion of your theory, Jonathon. Then what?"

"You'll marry me," he said with absolute confidence, "and we'll have a baby or two and live happily ever after."

Too bad she had thrown the dismembered tail in the wastebasket on the way out, Leah thought. He was certainly deserving of another whack or two. His timing was deliberate and perfect; she couldn't say anything with Bea in earshot, lounging on a pile of lumber in the back of the truck.

Seven

Leah's potting wheel back in Boston had an electric motor with three speeds and a cushioned seat. When she'd sold it, it had gathered ten years worth of dust. Setting up her bargain wheel from Charlie Cranberry, she couldn't help compare the two and see how symbolic of all the changes they were: from top of the line to starting from scratch, from the Space Age to the Stone Age.

Jonathon moved her acquisition into place in the big drafty shed in the back yard. He took off the canvas tarp. "You sure you want to work out here? The basement's bigger."

She crouched, inspecting the heavy stone flywheel at the base. A couple of weeks of kicking to drive the wheel and she expected spectacularly muscular legs. "Did you ever see a potter at work, Jonathon? There will be a royal mess of spattered slip and clay. Out here, I'll get fresh air and no guilty conscience if I don't clean up."

The seat was a battered, scooped tractor part. The blackened metal was cool to her touch even in June. Leah sat down gingerly and looked around, an unexpected excitement starting in the pit of her stomach. It had been years and years; what if she had forgotten everything?

In the corner, the clay in barrels was conveniently stowed. There was a rough table for wedging clay, a hole in the tar-paper roof to admit sun and missing boards in the walls to let the breeze blow through. Beatrice had taken care of the spider webs and sent Tipsy Jane through on mouse patrol.

"A studio!" Leah exclaimed with a nervous laugh. "Primitive but it's mine.... Thanks for your share in hauling and dragging and discarding. By the way, what did you finally do with the Cranberry Collection?"

Jonathon smiled and dusted off his hands. "I sunk the lot off Spring Bay. In a few hundred years, some diver will announce he found a treasure trove of ancient art. Well, you get going. I can see your fingers twitching. I'll pick Bea up and bring her home in time for dinner."

"She'll have driven your father crazy long before dinner," Leah said, busy tying her hair back with a rolled bandana. "And at the going rate, she'll have to paint every lobster buoy in Maine and Massachusetts to earn her boat money."

"Don't discourage private enterprise," admonished Jonathon, with a wink. "Joe already gave her a raise from three cents to a nickel apiece. He's got a captive audience for his tall stories."

He gave Leah a short wave and ducked out of the squat building, ready to leave without further ado. Leah jumped up and followed him into the yard.

"Hey, what about you?" she asked. "Are you staying for dinner tonight? You should have the honor of seeing my first efforts. I wouldn't be preparing to sink up to my elbows in clay if it wasn't for you."

"I thought you'd never ask." Jonathon stepped closer and put his arms around her waist, leaning back to smile approval at her grubbiest shirt and jeans. "I'm afraid I might be wearing out my welcome."

"No, I'll be sure to tell you if you are." She tilted her face up and saw his smile broaden. He knew he wasn't going anyplace without kissing her. His every arrival and departure was marked by a kiss, sometimes light and sometimes passionate.

His vigor today was remarkable, and Leah held on, reluctant to let him go. Courting, Jonathon-style, meant lots and lots of affection, including kisses, hugs, touches and compliments. She frankly adored it but he also made it clear that his restraint had the upper hand.

"Go to it, tiger," he said, ending the kiss and giving Leah a playful jab on her chin. "Good luck!"

"Luck has nothing to do with it. This is skill, talent, practice." Leah gave him a feeble wave, wishing she felt as confident as she sounded.

She could have stood there much longer, comforted by his embrace, the sturdy, solid feeling she got when they held each other. But it was probably better that Jonathon exercised such careful control. More kisses and more time, and she inevitably began to get the little stabs of excitement, the lightning flashes of arousal.

All this energy darting around like static electricity had an outlet, safe and well grounded. Leah walked back to the shed, taking deep breaths of the salt-tinged morning air. No one was around, she assured herself. If her boasting was just that, idle and empty, she had no one to blame but herself and no witnesses.

She dug out a sizable lump of sticky gray clay and hefted it. Even the weight and texture were awkward after so long. Slamming the mass down on the table and kneading it was better. It occurred to her that she would have vented a lot more of her anger, the disillusionment and disappointments, of the past two years if she'd wedged clay before this.

In an hour, she was not perspiring. She was sweating. With incredibly grungy fingernails that required unmerciful clipping, Leah flipped on Bea's portable radio and sang at the top of her voice. Maybe she could still throw a pot and maybe she couldn't, but at least no neighbor was going to knock on her floor with a broom handle and stifle her vocal creativity.

The basic skills, the correct patterns of motion and the sequences, were still there. Leah was tired and aching before the day was over but essentially pleased. It was frustrating only to remember how easily she had done this once, unconsciously. Her hands and brain knew what to do, but there was a clumsier, slower rhythm to her work. The simplest step, centering the lump of clay, took a long struggle. It was exertion. It was work.

Jonathon's coffee mug was a project for some very distant day. She had only succeeded in raising a wall of clay straight up and smashing it back down. Her legs weighed tons from the effort of driving the wheel at a constant speed. She was mucky and damp, covered with the evidence of her occupation.

It wasn't until she recounted the day to Jonathon and Bea that something different, something new occurred to her.

"I'm bushed," Leah admitted. "I'm four thumbs and a finger on the wheel but today was great! I can hardly wait to get up tomorrow and jump in my wallow. I'm ... I'm happy!''

''That's a start!''

Jonathon's expression was bland, but she sensed there was more to his phrase than simple congratulations on her reborn interest.

He gave her a Mona Lisa smile and sang, ''This could be the start of something big,'' until Bea drowned him out with a Lupo and the Wolves cassette.

''There are precisely eleven children in my age group in this entire district!'' Bea arranged another generous portion of casserole on her plate. ''The bus ride to Kildear Middle School takes twenty-five minutes. Longer in the winter, sometimes. And ... are you ready for this? Barnaby Templeton tried to tell me it wasn't bad. Not bad? They actually have to help and push or dig out the bus when it gets stuck.''

''Terrible,'' said Leah. ''Shocking! I'm sure there's a violation of child labor laws in this somewhere.''

Bea nodded, her mouth too full of noodles to speak. Her appearance had undergone a further modification in the past week. Scarves and dangly earrings proved a nuisance when Bea was painting lobster buoys for Joe Wardwell, and rowing in the mornings was chilly, so Bea had totally abandoned her wardrobe of flimsier, glittery shirts. The only paint on her tonight was a generous spattering of white and orange enamel, matching her high neon-orange sneakers.

''I didn't know you and Barnaby were buddies,'' Jonathon said casually. His face and voice were serious, but a blue glint flashed at Leah from the depth of his eyes. ''Nice kid, isn't he? Let me think. He plays soccer, is interested in seabed mining and usually has a set of earphones stuck on his head."

"He's okay, I guess," Bea replied. "I don't know about the rest but he has decent taste in music . . . for Fairharbor. He turned up his tapes the other day while we were both working on the pier. He didn't say two words to me. Of course, your dad was busy telling me about this mermaid he once caught."

"No blue hair, leather bands with nail heads?" Leah clucked her tongue. "Someone must take this town in hand and raise the level of popular culture, Jonathon. When people find out children are required to do chores and some women here still wear girdles, but all of them wear bras, the press will want to expose the place time forgot."

"You don't wear a bra every day," Bea said. "What's a girdle? Have I ever seen one?"

Dinners hadn't ever been like this, Leah thought, during Jonathon's vivid description of his grandmother's corsets and his mother's girdles. Bea was convulsed with laughter, asking questions and not believing any of the answers, mermaids and girdles being equally exotic topics to her. Instead of being glued to the television or rushing off at the first opportunity, she was content to snicker into her applesauce.

Leah's custom of fixing a hasty, simple afterwork meal was becoming a thing of the past. She was cooking more but also, secretly, enjoying it. There was time during the day to drag out a cookbook and experiment, and her audience was more appreciative. More often than not, Jonathon was there, adding his commentary, giving his opinions and livening up the evenings.

"Girls padded their chests?" Her daughter stopped eating to smooth her T-shirt over the flat plane of her own nonexistent bosom. "With what?"

"My sister had a pair of my crew socks she was partial to," Jonathon confided. "I know it sounds funny to you, but a big chest used to carry more, pardon the pun, weight then."

Try as she might, Leah could not imagine this discussion going on with Michael. Beatrice was versed in facts that Leah had had to pry out of her friends at a much later age and was virtually unshockable, superficially more sophisticated and glib, but she was woefully ignorant of other times and styles. Jonathon listened and didn't patronize. He didn't lose patience with Bea's ramblings and affectations or lie or ignore her.

He's always at ease, always himself, Leah realized with an admiring smile in his direction. There was no difference between a Jonathon at work or a Jonathon relaxing, no such thing as company manners or professional facade. Assessing him as a rather simple, ordinary man had been her biggest mistake; she was beginning to suspect he was extraordinary and deep, a complex person without confusions.

"He's twelve," Bea said suddenly, without bothering to name her subject. "He was scraping barnacles off a hull. Do you think I should ask him over to listen to my Burning Itch tapes, Mom?"

"Ask him," Leah agreed with a smile. "I can stuff cotton in my ears and wrap a muffler around my head, but it's possible that Barnaby Templeton has as little regard for his hearing as you do. Ask Bethany and Olivia, too. I'd just as soon make one big batch of cookies as several."

"Cookies! How hopelessly domestic," sneered Bea. "You really are, Mom. Face it! Being around a house all day is ruining you. No makeup, no panty hose. You like a new recipe as much as playing with the clay."

"I'm cut to the quick," Leah said lightly, starting to clear dishes. "Luckily, we've rooted out my problem before it became chronic. We'll go back to boil-in bags and sanity soon, honey. And thank goodness domesticity is not genetic. You'll never have to enjoy fixing a meal that everyone eats."

Jonathon smothered a laugh with his napkin and took over the clearing. "Tell us what's happening in the shed. You won't let us watch you work. At least give us a hint."

"Chocolate chip is all right," Bea said dreamily. "But no *milk*!"

"I'll check the wine cellar for a nice carbonated soda," Leah promised. She launched into her difficulties in the potting shed, detailing her air bubbles in the clay, the greater effort it was taking to get back into the groove as a potter.

Jonathon listened to her as if it mattered to him. She understood, relating her woes and minor triumphs, that dinner had become a nightly forum, a new ritual. That knowledge was pleasant; she could try to hold on to it when she and Bea went back, keeping one meal as an important time to share their respective days. But the pleasure wasn't unalloyed.

She was going to miss him. The certainty filled her with a dread. They weren't truly, fully lovers, only friends who had shared a single night. And she was going to miss him horribly. It wouldn't be any worse if they were conducting a blazing affair—or would it? The idea that she loved him haunted her every day as much as memories of his making love to her flared up during certain nights.

Jonathon was laughing to himself in the kitchen. She would remember the muffled sound and the way he helped without making any fuss, and his walk, both typical of Fairharbor and unique to him. There was a special glow to these simple dinners and conversations because of him, and Leah was ready to admit, if only to herself, that the glow was love, starting to burn brighter, too incandescent to hide much longer.

"You quit," he threatened without menace, "and I'll throttle you if you ever say 'ship' to me anymore. When you put a decent piece of stoneware on my workbench, we'll talk turkey, woman."

"Hey, I didn't say I was throwing in the towel. I'm just complaining because it's more trouble than I planned on."

Love was something she hadn't planned on. She didn't want any more complications. *Love*, buzzed a strong current of feeling when his hand sought hers across the table. *Love*, her blood sang dangerously loud, when he kissed her or watched her intently with his earnest eyes.

"I don't know quite what to do," she heard herself saying. The problems with making inert clay obey her was not the trouble she had in mind, however. She had tried out the sound of the plain and simple truth in her head and it was echoing in there, a hollow, persistent but unspoken cry.

Jonathon, I love you.

"Can I be excused?" Bea moaned. "And I've gotta use the phone. I'm going to call Barnaby and find out if he likes Burning Itch."

"You are a modern, liberated girl," said Leah. "Call."

"You've got more wash on that line than a woman with ten children," Jonathon called. He came through the hedge and watched Leah, clothespins in her mouth, hang up another pair of jeans.

She bent down and held out one of his old shirts, her usual outfit lately. "Spare me the humor," she said, snapping a clothespin in place. "I'm feeling sorry for myself and I don't want you to spoil it. I wash every other day, I don't have a dryer like a civilized lady, and I can't take the time off to run to Suds 'n' Duds. I'm too busy making lopsided bowls and teapots with lids that don't fit."

"Discouraged?" He came over and started on the other line. "Thinking of giving up?"

"Yes," she replied. "I made one decent cup in two weeks and used fifty pounds of clay to get there."

"Depressed, eh? I've got the cure. How about a picnic, you and me communing with Nature at Powhatan Meadow. You can dig clay or scream and bitch. No one for miles!"

Leah hesitated and then bobbed her head up and down. "All right! You don't have to listen to my griping. I'll talk to squirrels at this point."

She had an even better reason to accept. A break, an airing was fine, but the prospect of the two of them being alone was very attractive. Without interruption or intrusions, she was planning to tell Jonathon how truth wasn't always a fixed star, a stable element. In the past two weeks, her feelings had changed and grown like the malleable clay she held on her wheel. Her feelings for him were recognizable as love, shaped by all the time they spent together—stronger, higher, wider feelings that assumed a form and needed to be shown, not merely explained.

Love was a strange, beautiful object, and she wasn't about to crush and push it back down into a shapeless mass, the technique she used with most of her creations. But, Leah thought nervously, she wasn't prepared to promise Jonathon more. Talk of marriage was premature and childish. She was not sure she would always feel this way. She didn't expect him to love her always. She could show him how often a wonderful, seemingly perfect piece of unfired greenware cracked while it was drying, or broke in the kiln. By now he knew how "perfect" a marriage she and Michael had dissolved.

How many times had she been warned that when something seemed too good to be true, it probably is? Jonathon and her feelings for him fell in that category.

"Peanut butter and jelly, stale potato chips and a thermos of iced tea," Leah sang out as she emerged from the house. She held a paper bag and the plaid container aloft. "Want to reconsider your hasty offer? Or stop somewhere for a box of fried chicken?"

"I'm a simple man with simple tastes," Jonathon said. He hoisted the empty barrel and two shovels into the truckbed while she got in. "Your company in the countryside was the big attraction. You've been cooping yourself up in the studio too much. That's why you can't see the ceramic forest for the trees and decide what to do. Let's look at a couple of real trees, get some blisters digging clay and squash ants."

"Okay, sounds good." Leah unrolled her window and hung her head out slightly, letting the wind make a mess of her hair. "I never played hookey when I was a kid. I didn't think I'd pick up bad habits from you, of all people. Bea, yes. You? No."

"Once I went five years without a full day off," Jonathon said. "Once, no more. I'm my own boss, so I gave myself the rest of today for a picnic."

She caught the reference to his unknown past and tucked it away. That was the most she ever got—a vague allusion, a tiny hint of a life before this one, as if he was reincarnated. More than anything else it was unsettling. She doubted that Jonathon was a major criminal or that he'd made more mistakes in his life than she had. Friends and lovers should not keep secrets, except their own shared ones.

"You remember when you told me that not everything had to be spoken?" She stared out at the roadside stands of pine, fresh green at their tops, shadowed and cool at their dark, hidden bases. "It was the first night you and I kissed. Really kissed!"

"I'm not likely to forget any time I've kissed you," he said happily. "Sometimes it still seems like the first time."

"You work hard but you take off when you like," Leah plunged ahead. "To fish, to work on Bea's boat, to do whatever takes your fancy. I thought you had a big cabinetwork order for the new house in Spring Bay. But I was down in the mouth and you can just go.... How?"

He shifted his eyes to her and back to the dirt road. "The deal fell through. They went with ready-made cabinets and canceled any custom work."

"Not just today. We went to the beach last week. The week before, you went on errands for me to get glazes and pick up Amos Bentley's carvings. Spur-of-the-moment trips. No planning, really. And you don't sound upset about losing the Spring Bay job, Jonathon. It's as though money doesn't mean anything to you."

"There's no fast lane to live in around Fairharbor," he reminded her needlessly. "I've got all the hammers, saws and drills I can use."

She was not giving in this time, swerving off the subject to avoid offending him, the way he wheeled the truck around a bad spot in the road.

"You live simply but well, Jonathon. There's the house, your boat, this truck. And yet, you charge ridiculously low prices for top-quality work. I hear things in the post office. I heard them at the box auction. You do a lot of work that you don't charge for at all. I offered you big bucks for one of your model ships. What was my last figure? Forty-eight hundred dollars? And you, correct me if I'm wrong, fell off the couch, laughing, snorting coffee.... Tell me how you can afford to sneeze at money, play when the spirit moves you!"

"I'm rich," he said. There wasn't any flicker of light in his eyes and his lips weren't twitching with suppressed humor.

Leah peered at him, waiting for the rest of the joke to follow. "Oh, sure! And I'm Princess Di."

"Is this stuff really important to you?" Jonathon asked, irritated. He flipped the sun visor down impatiently and bumped the truck off the rutted dirt into Powhatan Meadow.

"Yes," said Leah vehemently. "I'm not interested in borrowing money or telling you how to run your life. I'm interested in *you* and why there are certain subjects that are off limits, taboo. You will talk openly about almost anything but yourself."

"You used to be married to a man who talked about nothing but himself," Jonathon said coldly. "In the long run, did you really know him?"

"You!" Leah tapped his chest with her forefinger. "Not me, not Michael, not Bea. I want to know why I know so little and feel so much for Jonathon Jericho Wardwell."

The hum of the cicadas rose and fell, and a few unseen ducks broke into their chorus with raucous squawks. Jonathon sat, pensively quiet, before he gave a short, resigned nod and opened his door.

"Okay, let's go review more Wardwell history but less interesting than the rest, if you insist. I just didn't think you'd be more inclined to love me more, or less, for that matter, by hearing about who I was . . . what I was."

"I won't be," Leah said, but before she could add, *because I already do love you,* he was gone. Jonathon hauled out the blanket, the lunch and was stalking away through the grass.

She ran to catch up with his hurried stride. By the time she scrambled over a low stone wall, he was spreading the blanket under a tree near the stream's bank. He propped himself against the trunk, looking easy and relaxed, but when Leah sat down to face him, she saw the telltale signs of tension. His brow was creased, his fingers so tightly interlaced around one knee that his knuckles were bleached, and a darkness had invaded his eyes.

"You'll understand," Jonathon said without any other preamble, "but I hope to God you won't care about my history. As confined and annoying as this town can be, multiply your feelings by a hundred, a thousand, and you'll know why I left. How could I amount to anything or be anybody important here?"

He talked faster than she'd heard him speak before, a clipped, staccato delivery, and the more he talked, the less like Jonathon he looked. It was eerie; Leah watched his features freeze into a hard mask, not his usual deadpan when he kidded but an older face devoid of feeling.

"Power. Money," Jonathon spat out. "I learned where those commodities were marketed and I went out to get them. That's why I went to Harvard and why I majored in Economics. And I was very good, highly successful."

"You are, at everything," Leah added quietly.

He smiled, a thin smile she was chilled by. "It wasn't enough. I wasn't content with an education, a living, or my escape from small-town mentality and mores. Like old Josiah Wardwell, I was out to be the best, at any cost."

Leah found it necessary to pour herself some iced tea. Listening to Jonathon describe how cold-blooded he was, long ago, made her mouth dry and her throat ache. The man he told her about was so totally different from the one she knew that she could not help thinking of Dr. Jekyll and Mr. Hyde.

"I had a passing interest in politics," he said, "but I had a real talent in high finance. I went to Wall Street, the capital of big money and power, and established myself as a resident financial wizard. Investment analyst!"

Briefly, Jonathon explained the ins and outs of high-risk ventures, how much pressure he lived with, how costly any mistake was. The incongruity of the pastoral setting, fleecy clouds passing overhead and no one else for miles, struck her when he detailed the staggering sums he dealt in, the constant, barely controlled madness of his job.

"Five years!" Jonathon passed his hand over his face and shuddered. "But I was the best, Leah. Or so the people who counted told me. I'd made fortunes for them and amassed a tidy sum for myself. I was paying more for a parking space and a showy apartment than I make in a year in Fairharbor."

He stopped, and Leah was afraid he wasn't going to go on. "You mentioned Josiah and his drive to be the best. He didn't make it and you did, it sounds like. What happened?"

He smiled and was Jonathon again, leaning to take the thermos top from her and swigging down the rest of the tea. "Joe Wardwell came up to the Big Apple to invite me to go fishing," he finally said with a chuckle.

"I don't understand," Leah admitted.

"Well, I didn't, either, at first. We hadn't had much communication since I spoiled his plans for a lobster empire by leaving for college. He showed up in Manhattan, trying to fast-talk the doorman of my building who took him for a vagrant."

Leah could picture the grizzled, weathered senior Wardwell and she grinned, too. Joe didn't take no for an answer, a trait he had obviously passed on to his offspring. He would attend a White House dinner wearing his "lucky" argyle socks.

"You dug out a rod and reel, went with him and never went back to mega-money dealings?"

Jonathon invited her closer with a gesture and settled her under his arm, tucking her head onto his shoulder. "I showed him everything I'd accumulated from a closet full of tailored suits and Italian shoes to the keys to the Porsche. I showed off my current woman. I didn't have much free time, so I picked them by looks. They didn't have to be able to say or do much, just stand around and be the most beautiful accessory."

"And you propose marriage to *me*?" Leah stroked the fine lines at the corners of her green, bewildered eyes. "I'm not jealous, merely astounded. Your standards really changed; some would say dropped."

"No," insisted Jonathon, tracing the same little creases and pausing to kiss them. Then he held her very tightly and erased most of her doubts with a less tender, much longer kiss. "You are the best. I still want the best. Ten years ago, I figured out what that meant before I repeated history and ended up like Josiah. Burned out and convinced that what I didn't have was more important than what I had.''

"What's best?" she asked softly, unable to resist nibbling his lower lip.

"I won't be able to tell you if you keep that up," Jonathon whispered hoarsely. "I'll be forced to show you..."

Leah took her mouth away from his, but she kept her hands linked around his neck. "I'll try to behave. I goaded you into talking, after all. I want to hear the whole story."

"I neglected to mention my best ulcers, insomnia and an unending, nagging fear. I was the best, but when would a better financial gunslinger come to town? It was inevitable, my dad pointed out. I was the guy they were all shooting at, when they weren't shaking my hand. I couldn't rely on anyone else or on myself alone forever; I'd make mistakes and fall from favor, or run into the younger, sharper whiz kid.''

"I fell from favor by relying on someone else," said Leah. "I want to be self-reliant and self-sufficient more than anything else, I think."

"Then power and money can't be the only measure," said Jonathon very authoritatively. "Other people's opinions, either. I came back with the old man to fish and take a deep breath without looking over my shoulder. I ended up doing odd jobs to keep my hands busier than my mind and realized how much I liked it, how happy I was. I knew when I was doing my best and when I wasn't; it was a feeling, not a bonus check, and it didn't make me crazy."

"Is this a variation of the 'less is more' theory?" Leah inquired. "You gave up—"

He gripped her shoulders and wouldn't let her finish. "I gave up nothing! I didn't give up love or laughter or friends. I didn't give up a family, a wife and children, the way so many of the men around me did to be number one with a corporation."

Leah flopped down on the blanket and stared up into the branches of the tree overhead. It was so quiet, she thought, so incredibly peaceful. The lacy leaves were in constant motion, but they swayed slowly, gracefully, not frantically. She could hear the wind moving through them, the grasses on the bank, and the occasional splashing of water in the stream.

The heat made her feel loose limbed and sleepy. She stretched and closed her eyes, letting the warmth soak into her, blocking out the too-bright flash of the sun through the leaf canopy.

"Beautiful," she sighed contentedly when Jonathon joined her. "You can leave me here for a while and come back later. I needed this break. What a fantastic day!"

"Maybe I will," Jonathon said. "You look relaxed, happy. When I first saw you, you both were drawn, kind of pinched and jumpy. Now there are roses in your cheeks..." He stroked her face gently, a touch as tender and sweet as the breeze itself. "You're a beautiful woman, Leah."

She opened her eyes, seeing him as if it was the first time. "You've been wonderful," she whispered slowly, "more considerate and caring than anyone I've known. If you think there's been improvement in Leah, you should take credit for it. I never felt particularly beautiful, especially talented or outstanding but I don't feel ordinary when we're together."

He plucked a long strand of grass and ran it over her face, tickling her chin. "You're going to make me blush.

Why don't we say we're glad we met each other and leave it at that?''

She hoisted herself onto one elbow and stopped the hand wielding the weed. The blouse pulled tight across her chest and she saw his eyes flick downward, move as swiftly back to her face.

"Because that's not enough," she said thickly, "for either of us. We've been getting closer, in every respect except one. There hasn't been a day in the last few weeks we haven't shared some part of...but not a single night."

"You know why." He took his hand from under her fingers and let it fall onto his thigh. "It's heaven and hell being with you. It's plain hell when I'm not with you."

"I wish I could say what you want to hear," Leah whispered. "I have to tell you what's real, what feels right to me. You're special to me, Jonathon, and you always will be."

He leaned forward to place a kiss on her mouth. Leah took the kiss but she also put her hands on his shoulder, pulling him down with her until he was stretched out, held close.

"I want to show you what I feel," she said. "I love you. I can't tell you what's going to happen because I don't know. But I finally understand what's happened. I love you."

"Tell me again." He unbuttoned the top of her shirt and put his lips on her throat, finding the pulse there. "Tell me slowly. We have all day. We can have until the end of time, if you like, if you'll decide to stay with me."

"I . . . love . . . you," Leah whispered, feeling his hands begin to move, the flutter of his breath and fingers.

Eight

Leah shut her eyes. The slow trail of his kisses along her neck stirred the deepest longing she'd ever known. The weeks of being with him and yet not being with him fully had honed her desire into the sharpest, sweetest edge.

"I was beginning to think I'd never hear you say it," Jonathon sighed, his mouth brushing her ear.

"I didn't think I would." She gasped softly when his hand slipped under her blouse, gliding over the breast he released from the pressure of his chest.

"Love me or tell me?" Jonathon rocked back slightly, keeping their lower bodies in close embrace, allowing himself free rein. His fingers roamed, drew teasing circles and captured the hard nipples.

"Both," she moaned.

Her eyelids fluttered open for an instant, saw the naked expression of his own love and excitement and closed quickly. But she could not shut out the dizzying surges of sensation that raced in her at the pressure of his legs and stirring flesh. And as Jonathon unbuttoned her blouse and lowered his mouth to her breasts to tantalize and taste, she knew she could not shut him out of her life, keep her heart isolated and safe.

"Let me love you slowly, the way it should be. No rush. No hurry." His lips showed her what he meant, beginning to move toward her stomach, his fingers unsnapping her jeans and spreading the fabric.

"Jonathon, we're out here in the open," Leah protested feebly.

"This is where we want to be—in the open. Always . . . with each other."

"Someone could—"

"No, this isn't Boston," he whispered, unlacing her shoes and taking them off. He tugged at each pant leg and her jeans followed.

She twisted, lifting her hips, but it was to help, not hinder him. The heat in her blood made her skin tingle, and she needed to feel the breeze and his damp kisses more than clothes. Her own fingers were flexing, eager to pull away the last barriers between them.

When she was nude, Jonathon was gently adamant and still dressed, pushing her shoulders back to the blanket.

His mouth touched hers briefly and Leah's arms reached to hold, her finger stretched into his hair. He pulled away before she could persuade him to settle his weight on her. His eyes were fever bright, blue fire dancing, as he looked down and touched her, with slow admiration, lingering strokes. His glance caressed as thoroughly as his eyes, seeing the effect of his hands' lazy explorations take hold of her.

"Oh, God, I want . . . I want . . ." Her head rolled from side to side as her hips began their own restless motion, seeking the incredible sensations.

"I know you now. I know what you want," Jonathon groaned. "That's what all the waiting was for."

"Don't wait," she begged, arching wildly. "Oh, please, don't."

Her pleas went unheeded. Instead, Jonathon bent over her and retraced the path his hands had wandered, licking and nibbling, the damp suction of his mouth and sweep of his tongue leading her to a wild and wanton abandonment.

Mindlessly she let the exquisite spiraling feelings take over. His shoulders nudged her legs wider apart. His parted lips lowered to search her and ultimately to give more and more pleasure with a shocking ardor but a very profound tenderness.

The meadow rang with her sharp cry of release, but Leah was no longer conscious of where they were. Nothing mattered and no place was lovelier than the white-hot light surrounding and invading her. She trembled with the bursting of the light; the explosion racked her body and splintered the white into a crazy quilt of brilliant colors.

She lay still, floating freely in the sunlight and feeling the breeze wherever it blew across her moist skin. Little aftershocks made the muscles of her stomach ripple and tighten and she flung her arm across her face, amazed at the acuteness of her own release, vaguely appalled at the realization of how selfish the moment had been.

"Jonathon, it's over and you never . . ." She could hear the shaky quality to her voice, the regret.

"It's not over," he contradicted. "This was only the beginning for us, Leah."

His emphatic statement, with a quiet, sure tone made
her look at him. He was stripping off his clothes with deft
motions. Leah raised her head slightly and passed her
hand across her face. She wiped away the blur of tears
formed in passion and pushed back her tangled curls of
hair.

He was fully aroused and he smiled very slightly when
her gaze swept his body. Haste had made waste the first
time they made love; she didn't realize how remarkable his
physique was. "At least I never was shy. Not like...that.
You seem to bring out the worst...or is it the best?"

"Best," he confirmed, coming toward her. The rise and
fall of his sun-dappled skin was deeper already, anticipating the next stage of their discovery of each other.

She would have sworn he'd drained her of all energy, all
excitement, but the scent and sight of his body made the
pulse in the base of her throat quicken. When he was close
enough to touch, standing above her, Leah stroked upward along his legs, delighting not only in their firmness
and the male textures of skin and hair alone, but in the
yearning sway of his torso and the involuntary response
of his muscles.

He sank slowly to his knees while her fingers caressed
and explored. He was beautiful, the most passionate and
controlled lover she could have fantasized about. She
wished she was as bold and skilled. She wanted to be the
best lover for him, the best woman for herself.

"I'd like to..." Leah hesitated, not shy but not sure how
bold to be. The tip of her tongue darted out and moistened her lower lip.

"I'm yours," Jonathon said, breathing harder. His eyes
narrowed and his face was drawn taut with need. "Do
whatever you like...but soon...oh, that feels good, so
good."

With a groan that shook his body and vibrated through her, Jonathon lay down, the length of his body given up to her kisses. Covering him inch by inch with eager lips made him gasp and clutch at her, but her daring also fed a renewed aching in her loins.

Whatever she had experienced with Michael, whatever she had known before was a distant memory. This was real and wonderful and right. She felt as if she and Jonathon had invented love and they were the first people to share it, so nothing was wrong.

"Oh, God!" Jonathon's hips were lifting, seeking more of her. "Leah . . . soon, love."

She understood his soft warning and the union he was hungry for without having to think about it. Balanced over him, Leah moved easily and naturally to guide his hard flesh into joining hers. The wonder of taking him deeply into the heated core of her body was a reflection of the place he held in her feelings, the secret and sensitive center.

Jonathon was saying her name over and over in time with the lift and thrust of her hips. His fingers held and released the curve of her waist, then the roundness of her buttocks with the same rhythm. His eyes were open, a dizzying blue rim around a very tiny black iris, and hypnotic, intent on her face.

"Now," he said very slowly and clearly. "Now."

He strained up as Leah slid down, intent only on giving him the same joyful release she had gotten. Unexpectedly, with an intensity that made her fall forward and hold him, her body was swept with the uncontrollable, unending release once more. She bit her lips, blocking the whimpers of her ecstasy, but he knew. And Jonathon shared with her an explosive moment that was far different from a physical outpouring alone but a meshing of souls, as well.

They rested together, listening to the birdsongs. The thunder of his heartbeat under her ear had rolled away to a regular and steady sound. Jonathon put his hand in easy, intimate possession on her hip, caressing the soft, untanned skin over the sharp rise of her pelvic bone.

"Nice spot for honeymooning," he said, breaking the spell.

"Please, don't." Leah sat up, reached for her clothes scattered around the blanket. She was not in the mood for a joke or another discussion of marriage.

Getting to the basic truths—his past, her love—was important. But those revelations did not magically alter every fact. She looked at him with love because she loved who he was, not who or what he had been, or because she harbored any illusion that he would change into the perfect man.

They wanted very different things, with the exception of each other. He had found his niche, while her search was just beginning.

"What if I got you pregnant?" Jonathon asked softly.

"You won't," Leah said. "I didn't take any chances. Babies are part of your plans, not mine, Jonathon."

She saw the expression of hope in his eyes die and had to look somewhere else. She could remember her keen longing for children as she told Jonathon why. Beatrice was going to be her first, not her only child, but it hadn't happened. Michael had claimed he needed her help as much as another baby would to launch his career, so they'd waited five years. When she was ready and he was established, he promised, the time would be right.

Then, the miscarriage. Leah lost a baby, weathered the trauma bravely, and would have tried again. But the last five years of her marriage were not good ones; Michael was polite and solicitous while he became an increasingly distant husband, an absent father. She should have guessed he was as busy at love elsewhere when he wasn't busy at law, but she didn't.

" 'The best laid plans of mice and men . . .' " He didn't finish his quote but trailed off into a whistle. "Hey, if you want us to dig clay, you better put clothes on. That pose of yours might spur me to action, but not with a shovel."

She was brought back from an unpleasant reverie and found her sock locked in a clenched fist, her nails curled into the flesh of her palm. No, babies were out of the question. Her priorities had shifted dramatically. She dressed quickly, even as Jonathon stood and watched her.

"Okay, I'm decent." She flashed him her brightest smile, refusing to let the past or the future intrude on the day, dimming the wonder of being together. "Soggy sandwiches or soggy business?"

"I'm at your disposal, madam," Jonathon said with a small, courtly bow. He straightened, smiling, but his eyes held a different, serious message. "Just don't dispose of me too quickly, too lightly."

"Don't be silly," Leah responded, running to put her arms around him and ruffle his hair. "Do you have any idea how difficult it is to find a man who laughs at my jokes, likes my cooking and volunteers to wield a shovel to advance 'Ahhht'?"

"Next to impossible, I'd say." He patted her behind affectionately. "And I won't let you forget it."

It was a good day. Leah already knew she wouldn't forget a single detail of it, any more than she would forget Jonathon. Today was special, set apart by his opening his past to her and her opening her heart to him.

* * *

"Okay, you guys, come on in!" Leah stepped away from the kitchen table and studied the overall effect of her arrangement. "The unveiling is about to begin."

There weren't many finished pieces in the lot, but it was only a start, she told herself again. What hadn't been mercilessly culled and thrown away was small in number but ambitious in scope. She beamed appreciatively at her teapot, with its snug-fitting lid and elaborate clay appliqué design. In another month, she could easily turn these out with ease, bigger and more brightly glazed.

Jonathon came in and just looked, walking slowly around three sides of the table. Bea had to heft every piece, upending each cup, plate and vase to see Leah's "chop," her distinctive incised mark, as if she was authenticating the goods.

"Three weeks, six objets d'art," Bea summed up cynically. "Hey, they're great, Mom, but it'll take years before we'll have service for twelve. And, at the rate I break dishes, sticking to plastic and paper plates is a better bet."

"Paper's wasteful and plastic tends to the ugly. Don't you like that cobalt blue with the wavy lines." Leah kept glancing at Jonathon, who offered no opinion.

"Very Scandinavian, looks like Wigren." Bea was extremely knowledgeable when it came to expensive furnishings like china, crystal and linen; she'd helped Karen pick out an entirely new household. "Are you going to buy things from yourself for Kate's gallery?"

Leah grabbed a tan, steepled casserole cover before Bea could wear it as a hat. "I wouldn't presume that far! This batch is not the best I can do, in the first place, and there isn't enough to sell profitably, secondly." She was hoping Jonathon would pipe up with praise and dispute her.

He went to the table, picked out a mug and a plate and came back to Leah. "I like these. They don't look like anybody else's. They look . . . *right*, somehow, to me. But what do I know?"

His selections were the two simplest, least adorned of her display. The white mug had been a lighthearted experiment. By gentle pressure, Leah's fingers had subtly changed the shape of the damp clay into suggesting a cat's sinuous form wrapped around the body of the mug. The handle was a tapering, lashing tail. The small plate, on the other hand, was as traditional an article as possible; Leah had fashioned a child's alphabet plate, incising the letters and numbers all around the rim and glazing it with a coarse salt.

"But what about this teapot?" She clutched his choices and jerked her chin toward the colorful, whimsically decorated object.

"You could show me how, technically or aesthetically, it runs rings around my favorites," he said with a slight shrug, "but I'd stick with these. I'm not convinced that cup isn't the best you can do. I don't see how it could be any better, any prettier or more functional. If it was a little bigger, I'd say you won a bet we had and take it home."

Leah cradled the cat mug and ran her fingers over the slightly raised curves and the flawlessly smooth surface. "Well, I was excited by the way it turned out, but a mug's not as showy as the teapot. And this mug's certainly not as commercially good as my jazzy blue one. It took a longer time to do and no one would buy, say, a set of white cats. They'd buy one!"

He gave her his widest grin. "See? One of a kind, special, unique, the best . . . and the plate, too."

"Oh, Jonathon, you're wrong! Every antique shop from here to Bangor has genuine alphabet plates: milk glass, pressed glass, porcelain. I've even seen them made out of wood. My own alphabet plate got passed on to Bea and it's stuck somewhere in a box, wrapped up in newspapers, for her crumb-crushers, if she ever decides to have children. I wanted to try something homely, humble."

"It is kinda homely," said Bea. "I thought kiddie things were always red or yellow, with rainbows or balloons. Not gray, white, blah! And a little kid can't read!"

"It's timeless," said Jonathon with a slight tone of awe. He held it up and rubbed his thumb on the neatly cut letters, the irregular but glassy crackle of the glaze. "This plate could be a hundred years old, handed down from one generation to the next. Think how pretty bright green vegetables would look on it! Carrots! Rainbows and balloons are nice but there's a message to the child who has an alphabet plate that's even nicer..."

"What?" Bea and Leah asked together.

"That being educated and literate is important, starting from his or her first little spoon of mush. That these symbols should be around every single day, a couple of times every day, until the child doesn't remember not knowing what an *A* looks like. And a baby will always associate the goodness of his meals with the alphabet."

"Wow!" said Bea predictably. "Heavy! Was that like subliminal advertising?"

"Yeah, I guess it was," said Jonathon. "Books and papers used to be expensive luxuries. A plate lasted a long time... if no one winged it across the kitchen."

"So you like my farthest-out experiment and my copycat antique," Leah said with a wry smile. "You'll never cease surprising me, will you?"

"I sure hope not. In fact, I plan not to," Jonathon commented, giving her a congratulatory kiss on the cheek. "When people can read each other like books, they're bound to get to the place where they aren't going to re-read the same page one more time. I haven't stopped being amazed at you!"

Bea seconded the motion, kissing Leah's other cheek. "You weren't just bragging, Mom. You're really good at this! Any other secrets I didn't know about?"

Leah made a point of not looking at Jonathon. "Well, besides my ballet training in Moscow and my Olympic medal in the hammer throw, no. Plain, ol', ordinary Mom. Oh, yes, and I'm taking up Mandarin Chinese next week."

"The language or the cooking?" Jonathon asked. "Fairharbor could use a Chinese restaurant. I doubt Peking will open an embassy here."

"You guys are nuts," Bea said, leaving them to such silliness.

"That isn't *our* junk!" Leah leaned on the porch rail while a troop of Bea's cronies assisted her in setting out a yard full of rummage. "We don't own a pink plastic flamingo. There was no painting on black velvet when we moved in, was there?"

"My partners and I collected more for the sale," Bea informed her, unloading cartons of paperbacks. "We're going to rake in the money, Mom. There's three garages', two attics' and a couple of sheds' worth here."

"Not those!" Leah ran down to rescue a chipped set of salt and pepper shakers, a gift from her own mother. "Partners? In what crime? Bethany Peacham, bring me that green cardigan sweater this minute. I don't care if it looks like a rag to you, Beatrice. I love it!"

"It is strictly bag lady fashion," said Bea, handing the item in question back. "I have signed notes promising to give time and turns in my skiff to any of the kids who brought items for sale."

"You don't own your time-share boat yet," Leah reminded her. "Your bank account in the First Mackey Flour Tin is still short by a considerable sum."

"I'll get it." Bea held up a lamp in one hand and a headless doll in the other like a boxer being announced the winner. "I'd have had the boat already, if Jonathon would have counted the allowance Daddy sends."

"Evil Jonathon," clucked Leah, "insisting you earn every cent on your own. Of course I have to say, in his defense, that he named a very, very, *very* reasonable price!"

One hundred dollars for a hand-built skiff was a gift, not a price. But Leah had been astounded at Jonathon's stipulation that Bea Rose was responsible—solely responsible—for raising the money. Contributions from Leah or Michael did not count, and Bea was sworn to an elaborate, salty, seafarer's oath that she would do it.

Leah strolled among the treasures littering her lawn and nodded sagely. "You might make it, kiddo. Let's hope everyone is in the buying mood and is dying for a..." She held up a pierced metal object; she had no clue as to what it was or did.

"A potato ricer," Jonathon shouted. He slammed the door of his pickup and came through the fence with an old trunk, high and round topped. "Wait'll you see the clothes in here! Arna had this stored in the attic. I'm afraid the cats will want it when they smell mouse tracks, but the dresses are a riot!"

"Is this kosher?" Leah asked him quietly. "You set a goal for her and then help her reach it by ferrying tons of discards here?"

"Sure, it's fair." Jonathon grinned. "I put an obstacle in her path. I'm giving her a hand pushing it out of the way. She could do it alone. She showed us that, sticking to the lobster buoy gig. But there's only five weeks left!"

"Five weeks?" Leah heard a hollow note in her own voice. It didn't seem possible that summer vacation was nearly over. The days had simply slipped away since she started working in the shed.

"That's not very long, is it?" He wasn't really asking a question but applying a touch of pressure to a sore spot. They hadn't brought up the issue of Leah's leaving and neither of them was particularly eager to start, but it ran like a cold current under other conversations.

"It's what we have," Leah said huskily. She walked away from him quickly, going to help Bea unpack a box of mismatched dishes, and feeling like a complete coward.

She could only postpone, not end, the inevitable clash with him. The kitchen calendar was marked in red, the days to pack and the day of departure circled. But August was still hidden under July, an unturned page.

The arrival of bargain hunters set the kids and Leah in motion. While Bea and her cohorts were in charge of the sales, she had volunteered to keep the potential customers happy with iced tea and lemonade. The front porch was designated as the concession booth, but before long there were as many people relaxing and socializing along its shadowed length as were wandering around the yard.

"I didn't expect every female under ninety to turn out," complained Leah. "They're still so standoffish with me, present company excepted." She handed Miranda another pitcher and stack of paper cups and gestured feebly with her chin toward the muffled babbling outside.

"Well, you best believe it wasn't my old Johnny Mathis records they showed up for," Miss Murching said. "You've got a crowd at your door because you haven't entertained before. They came to peek in the curtains and get more to go on than their fertile imaginations. I was thrilled myself at your neighborly gesture. You've kept to yourself, which was okay at first, but most folks were beginning to think you don't like us!"

"What?" Leah slammed the refrigerator shut and spun around. "Miranda, I get two, three people here every other day, delivering their handicrafts or showing me their stuff. I haven't put barbed wire across the road and yet, no one but you stops by for a social visit. I've assumed they'd passed judgment on me and kept away."

"There's a stupid assumption," Miranda said curtly. "I should have mentioned it sooner, I see, but I'm not a busybody by trade. The general feeling around and about is that you couldn't care less about Fairharbor people unless they show up with a rag rug in hand, ready to talk business."

Leah was stung, about to dispute Miranda, when she stopped and reconsidered. Helen Suds 'n' Duds had asked her to stop by; she hadn't taken the invitation seriously and acted on it. There were other vague "drop in" and "come 'round" suggestions, which Leah had dismissed as polite form. Had Mr. Windham's offhand instructions to his house to see the *Mayflower* been a sincere overture of friendship, not an afterthought?

Hefting another sweating glass jug of lemonade, Leah framed an apology along with her dozen best reasons. Miranda was hearing none of them. The postmistress expressed her opinion, as bluntly as ever, that no one was ever too busy to trade a good word.

"Business can be a reason or an excuse," Miranda declared. "I realize we put you off a bit at the outset, but the ball's been in your court for a while and you haven't done much."

"Time to serve, huh?" Leah smiled feebly. "I haven't meant to appear cold. One twenty-year hermit in the vicinity is more than enough."

Miranda chuckled. "See that Jonathon's been telling you our local lore. I keep warning him that he's liable to fill the position himself now that Skipjack Johnson's gone."

"Lighten up! I think he's been listening," muttered Leah as they went out with the refreshments.

The rest of the day took on a much different aspect. Leah was out of practice as hostess, but understanding what the draw to today's circus was helped her immeasurably. She made sure anyone who wanted a guided tour of Chandler House to see how she'd fixed it up was asked in. The latest consignments of items for Kate's gallery were brought out and shown off. Even her own meager output of pottery was handled and marveled over.

At several times there were more women sitting in the living room than wandering outside, picking through Bea's merchandise. Their initial tentative comments and attempts at conversation soon gave way to a gabfest, complete with decorating tips and childbirth horror stories.

When they finally left Leah wasn't surprised that she was more exhausted and hoarse than Bea and her sales force. Her pantry was a pound of coffee lighter and there wasn't a clean glass or a square of toilet paper left but it had been fun, a month's worth of "come by and set." She

staggered out to the porch to oversee the cleanup and was
promptly corralled by Jonathon.

"Put this on!" he demanded, slipping a rather musty-
smelling dress over her head. "Barnaby's gonna take a
picture of us before I haul Arna's wardrobe back. I can't
understand it. These clothes should have brought ten,
fifteen cents easy."

Leah blinked and took a good look at him. He was
wearing a frock coat so ancient that it was greener than
black in the sunlight. A yellow celluloid collar and derby
hat topped his outfit. She sneezed violently twice before
the dust in her garment settled, and she looked down,
surveying her costume.

Maroon velvet with bugle beads and sequins would not
have been her choice in July, but the spirit of dress-up and
silliness was infectious. She was too tired to object
strongly, anyway.

"Voilà!" Jonathon shook off a matching hat with be-
draggled white plume and arranged it on her head.
"Okay," he yelled to the children left milling around.
"Who's got the instant camera? Where's Bea Rose?"

"Spending the profits!" one of them shouted back.

"I'm here! I'm here!"

"Blow me down," swore Leah nautically, catching sight
of her offspring. "My daughter's first and only dress in
two years, and it's Heirloom City. I'll buy it!"

"Wrong era," frowned Jonathon, "but so what? I
thought you were putting on the sailor middy, Bea."

"This is better, more my style," argued Bea. She lifted
a long flounced chiffon skirt delicately in both hands as
if she had been born to wearing more formal attire and
swept up the steps regally. "Aren't I gorgeous? What a
dress!"

Leah gnawed the inside of her lip and tried not to blubber with maternal sentimentality. Bea did look wonderful, curiously grown up, in the white party castoff. "Frock," she corrected Bea. "And that one deserves the original name. Boy, oh, boy, I can really see how stunning you're going to be in a few more years. Barnaby, take a couple of extra shots, will you? I'll send Bea's grandmother in Maine one, if they turn out."

"Mrs. Mackey, my photographs always turn out," the lanky, fresh-faced boy said earnestly. "Now you sit in the glider and let Rosie get next to you. Jonathon, put your hand on Mrs. M's shoulder."

"Rosie?" Leah made a horrified gargling noise. "May lightning strike me if I allow anyone to call my daughter—"

"Sit down," interrupted Jonathon. "You're holding up the show."

Her baleful stares at Barnaby and Jonathon were wasted. The air of hilarity and chaos engendered by the whole day and the sale was captured on film while Bea giggled, Jonathon posed and joked, and a stray dog chased Tipsy Jane in widening circles amid trampled flowers and bags of leftovers.

Bea left the cat's rescue to her friends and went to hang up her "new" souvenir. Jonathon joined Leah on the glider, unpopping his stiff collar and sailing the derby back into Arna's trunk. Barnaby brought Leah the three pictures, smug in his skill.

"Very clear. Nice color," Leah acknowledged. "Unfortunately I look like I could bite the heads off nails." She laughed. "Jonathon, you seem to be in agony in this one."

"I think I'm rather distinguished in that. Or I could have been strangling for lack of air."

"What do I owe you, Barnaby?" Leah lifted her head and managed to stick her ostrich plume in the poor child's eye. "Oh, I'm so sorry! Let me get you an ice cube in a paper towel and a couple of dollars for the film. I'll be right back."

"No, no," Barnaby groaned. "That's okay, I'll add the cost of the pictures to my share in Bea's boat. Tell her I had to leave but I'll call her tonight for the final results."

"Love in bloom," Jonathon murmured softly as they watched Barnaby stumble off. "You nearly blinded your possible future son-in-law."

"Heaven forbid," sighed Leah. "Love in bud, maybe. But ten and twelve is a bit young, don't you think?"

Bea emerged from the house, flapping her tally sheet of the day's receipts, and it wasn't hard to guess her results.

"I'm about fourteen dollars short," she gleefully announced. "It's in the bag. It's a cinch. I can take Mrs. Edwards's twins to the park and paint buoys for the remainder."

"Come here," ordered Leah, squinting at the fist-sized object bouncing on Bea's chest as she capered around.

"I didn't do anything," Bea said, instantly subdued.

Leah crooked her finger. "I didn't accuse you of anything. Come here and let me see what you're wearing."

"Oh, this!" Bea picked up the silver chain Michael had sent in his last letter and dangled the wooden pendant. "Yeah, I swapped with some weird old man. Old, Mom! Old, old..."

"I get the idea," Leah said, examining the piece. "Go on."

"It was kind of neat. He wasn't any too sure where he was or how he got into our yard. He liked this pocket knife with a broken handle and he didn't have any money, just junk in his pockets. Did you ever hear of barter?"

"Ephraim," said Jonathon. "Uncle Ephraim. He's sweet and senile. I hope someone led him home."

"Buttons!" Leah forced Bea to take off her necklace and held up the chain to show Jonathon. "I listened to Miranda and was too quick to judge. Well, as buttons they're dismal failures, but don't you see the potential?"

Jonathon fingered the lumpy tan and brown button, painstakingly carved to conform to the natural contours of the gnarled driftwood and highly polished. It was approximately circular and there were holes drilled through the wood, but three holes were irregularly positioned.

"It's pretty," he offered. "Feels nice the way most wood carvings do. Are you going to sell them as a kind of worry stone?"

"Here's another one," Bea said, digging one out of her pocket. It was a silver gray, slightly smaller and covered with a tracery of delicate dark lines. "Kinda neat. There's no two alike."

"Perfect," declared Leah. "A man dropped by this week and tried to sell me his hand-tooled leather. I had to turn him down and I felt so bad. He really could have used the money, but his leather carving was strictly amateur and more Wild West in theme than Down East. But his belts were good leather, well cut and stained."

She set the wooden pendant swinging, outlining possibilities. Ephraim's wooden buttons fixed with thongs to a belt would be stunning. Or she thought Kate would be very interested in handling them as jewelry. They would make contemporary, natural accessories.

"The old man told me he had a peach basket full of them and I could go over and take some," reported Bea. "He says he uses them for checker games, too. Just picks out so many light ones and so many darker ones. They're all either browns or grays, I guess."

"On a leather checkerboard…" Leah was running ideas through, brainstorming. "Sure, why not? A chic conversation piece, a handsome gift."

"Ephraim Dowling, a celebrated artisan?" Jonathon howled with delight. "Well, why not? Grandma Moses did it."

"Was she the lady who bought the umbrella stand?" Bea asked. "She pinched my cheek, whoever she was."

Leah was happy to supply a short biography of the lady who began painting at seventy-six and won acclaim. Her little speech was as much to encourage herself to stick to her wheel as to inform Bea Rose. At the rate her work was progressing, Leah added, she'd be in her seventies before she was satisfied.

"There's always tomorrow," Jonathon noted philosophically. "You just get out there bright and early and practice the whole day. Bea and I will have final touches to put on her boat. We won't be bothering you!"

"Tomorrow I'm paying a call on Uncle Ephraim. I'll want Bea to go with me and make the introductions. After all, she appears to be his agent."

"What's my cut?" Bea said without hesitation, then retracted her statement. She generously extended his gray button to Leah. "Here, want it? If you find another one like it, they'd make a great pair of earrings."

"And here's a picture of you." Leah handed over the best of the three photos. "Go write your grandmother a letter and tell her all about the great sale, the dress, your boat, and how seven cats were profitably reduced to two. She'll love hearing from you!"

Bea was amenable. *Agreeable, pleasant,* Leah thought with a start. *We haven't done battle in nearly two weeks.* There had been a change, and whether it was vast and lasting or not, she was much more hopeful. Whether the change was due to something in the water or a natural process that would have occurred anyway mattered very little. Things were better, Bea was different, and Leah could find less fault and more things to praise and compliment Bea on lately.

Jonathon tipped up the edge of her velvet hat and planted a kiss on her ear, whispering, "You're really pleased with yourself, aren't you?"

"Sort of." She grinned and handed him the rest of the photographs to look at. "I told you about my grand design for this summer. My faith in myself is almost completely restored. Kate called me last night and is enthusiastic about the samples I sent ahead. Life with Bea has been better than bearable. And I'm in love. What more could I ask?"

Jonathon was too absorbed in the remaining shots of the odd trio to respond. He carefully picked his choice out, asking Leah for it.

"Sure, it's yours, but I don't want to see a wanted poster of us in Miranda's post office. Lord, we look slightly demented, all of us."

"We look like a family," Jonathon said abruptly. "I'd like us to be as much a family as possible."

"I don't know what you're talking about. We practically are, in some ways. You spend so much time with us, we do so many things together."

"What if I spend tonight here? The entire night . . ."

"Bea's not going anywhere this evening," Leah said.

"I know. I'm still asking if I could stay. Being a once- or twice-a-week lover, stealing a private hour now and then is okay, but I'd like to wake up holding you."

"Jonathon, we couldn't do that!" Leah was amazed that he would even make the suggestion to violate an unwritten, unspoken rule. "She'd know . . ."

"What? That we're lovers? That we're having an affair? I, for one, have no doubt that she's aware, on some level, of the situation."

Leah took off the ridiculous hat and dress, throwing them on the glider. She stood there, facing Jonathon, aghast.

"*This* from the man who refused to make love until very recently? When did you convert to a 'let it all hang out' attitude?"

"Never," he said succinctly. "Until we were committed to each other, this relationship couldn't proceed. Well, I love you and you love me. That fact made us lovers, however reckless and foolish. Bea's an unusually bright child and in many ways wise beyond her years. If there's anything Bea Rose recognizes above all else, it's basic facts and adult foolishness."

"No," said Leah firmly. "A flat no. You're talking about moving in. I feel as though you're pushing me into a corner. Are you ready to deliver an ultimatum, too? Live together openly or it's over? Marry me or else?"

His "No" came out very softly, unhappily. He stood up slowly and put his arms around her.

"I'm getting desperate, I think," Jonathon said. "I don't know how to bind us together any tighter but I have to keep trying. There must be some way to convince you to stay with me when summer ends; I have to find it."

"But don't spoil what we do have," whispered Leah. "Please!"

"I want to *keep* what we have," Jonathon said fiercely.

Nine

"Pull your guts out!" hollered Jonathon through cupped hands. "Show your mother what you can do!"

Leah squinted against the glare of sun on water and saw Bea's tiny hand wave at her. The skiff bobbed its agreement, too, on the gentle swells. It was a lovely, calm, nearly windless day, but Leah shifted uncomfortably and slipped her arm through Jonathon's.

"You sure she can get to Mark Point and back by herself?" she asked. "That's so far."

He gave Leah a sidelong glance and then shifted his attention back to the boat as it began to skim forward. Bea strained at the oars, looking very small and alone to Leah.

"See that?" His forefinger marked the passage. "I built it on dory lines, low and stable. The best boats ride up on waves and over. Bea won't get banged around in rough seas or swamped."

With a quiet, justifiable pride, he enumerated all the features of the *Jolly Rosie*.

Leah listened carefully to his list of extra oars and oar-locks. He'd supplied certain equipment, daggerboard and sprit rig, that enabled Bea to actually sail, not merely row. The skiff was wood, pine and oak with finishing touches of mahogany and teak. There wasn't a piece of plastic or fiberglass used in its construction; as well made as an antique, Jonathon claimed, the skiff would last a hundred years.

"Twelve feet doesn't seem very long from this distance," Leah said. The *Jolly Rosie* and her exuberant captain were rapidly becoming a small blotch on the sweeping expanse of water.

"She can handle that size best." He patted Leah's hand, and the iciness of her fingers must have alerted him. "Why, you're scared to death. Leah, she's quite capable, believe me."

She kept her eyes seaward, not daring to look at him. "I'm scared, yes. I'm sorry you two talked me into coming down to see the maiden voyage. I guess I've been imagining her paddling around in a lagoon or even on the Charles River. Damn, Jonathon, the ocean's *big*! And treacherous..."

"Oh, Leah," he said, hugging her into his side. "It's silly to worry, I'm telling you."

She bristled at his choice of words. "Silly? Look, you were into high-risk ventures, not me. She's not a seasoned sailor but a ten-year-old and my only child. Of course, I'm worried and protective."

"She can do it. She wants to be brave and independent...like you," Jonathon said in a much gentler tone. "Are you going to forbid her to row the boat she worked so hard to get? More important, are you going to limit this risk and force her to find another one to prove that she's growing up?"

"I don't want to hear or discuss this." Leah paced down the wharf and kicked the toe of her sneaker at some splintered planks. Bea was out of sight already, around the harbor, and Leah was busy mentally calculating how long it would take her to drive to the old lighthouse and wait there.

She turned back. "I'd like to drive out to Mark Point. Right now. A round trip isn't necessary to prove her point. She'll be aching and tired by the time she gets there."

"Halfway?" He shook his head. "You can do that, drive out and cut her success in two, if you want. I won't go with you, though. I believe in her ability, Leah. She's proving something to herself, not just to you or me."

"I don't want to hear about Josiah Windham Wardwell!" Leah shouted, letting her fear overpower her. "Bea doesn't have to be the best sailor in the world. I'd rather know she was safe."

"She can't be safe from everything," he retorted. "Neither can you! Nobody can guard against the arbitrary."

"Like the weather, the sea?"

"Like love and life," Jonathon said, equally provoked. "You're talking about being afraid for her but I hear something else. You've been bold and fearless starting your life over but only halfway brave when it comes to love . . . and me."

"It's Bea Rose I'm concerned about," Leah flung at him. She set off at a brisk pace toward Chandler House. If she had to walk back, pick up the station wagon and go herself, she would.

He called to her, loudly, angrily, and Leah lengthened her stride. She was right to worry and she wouldn't listen

to him anymore. Even on a placid ocean, under a cloud-
less sky, there were tricky currents and hidden rocky
shoals. She didn't need to have sailed these waters to know
there were dangers; her own life and common sense told
her—proof positive.

The low rumble of his truck's engine followed her. She
refused to look back or acknowledge his occasional shout
to get in.

Crossing streets to the other side did no good. Jonathon swung the pickup into the wrong lane and pro-
ceeded at five miles an hour. It was impossible to get
caught in traffic or to lose herself in Fairharbor.

"Okay," he hollered, "meet her there and show her,
louder than words, that you don't trust her! You don't
have confidence in her. Bea's found something good,
healthy and challenging, and you're determined to put a
limit on it. What's the worst that can happen? She'll tire
and put in on a beach and call us to come and get her. But
she'll try! She'll have tried and she'll try again another
day. You won't—"

"Pipe down!" Leah screamed at him and tried to smile
at the woman in the yard they were passing. "Hi, Alice.
Lovely day."

"Want me to call the police or the preacher?" Alice
grinned and waved at Jonathon. "Give him hell." She
followed Leah the length of her yard, hoping not to miss
a word.

Leah had to slow at the base of the hill up to the house.
The combination of shouting and marching was taking its
toll. Jonathon swerved over to the curb, letting the motor
run.

"Go away," she panted. "I do not want or need any
advice from you. I refuse to depend on you—or any
man—to tell me what to do."

"Fine!" Jonathon's snarl made her straighten up from the mailbox she was draped over. He stuck his head out of the passenger side window. "Except I wasn't speaking as your man but your friend.... Maybe you can't love and trust me completely, but I was hoping you'd demonstrate that faith in your daughter."

"How dare you?" Her head snapped up and emerald fire filled her eyes. "You don't know what's involved in raising a child, investing yourself in another person. You can't know what happens when complete love and trust is betrayed."

"I dare because I love you," he said slowly and clearly. "And I don't know because you won't allow me to, by inviting me into your life fully."

"Because this is finally *my* life, *my* child and *my* decisions!" Leah screamed, hearing how selfish and self-centered she sounded, not particularly caring.

"Then there's no room for me, literally or figuratively," he finished. "Get in! We're gathering a crowd. I'll take you wherever you want to go, except to Mark Point."

She did as he asked, embarrassed by the curious faces up and down the street, all her initial fear for Bea and anger at him dissolved into a sea of weariness. There was so little time left for them. Why did he insist on fighting and making the end bitter after these weeks of sweetness?

"Let's drive back and wait at the wharf," he suggested, as if the argument had never occurred. "I'm sorry I confused the issue by bringing you and me into it. Today's Bea's day, not ours."

His sincerity and contrition moved her as his anger could not. Perhaps she was overreacting, upset by the daring of her daughter, by Bea's self-confidence and independence. The very qualities she admired were scaring her. Would she be as frightened for herself or as quick to decide a challenge was too much for her to handle? Would she have forbidden a son to go for it?

Jonathon wasn't going anywhere, waiting for her decision. *My* decision, Leah thought, somewhat calmer. She had the final word, and it should be the right one.

"You really have a way of stretching me to my limits," Leah said sharply. "I haven't figured out how you do it, but it keeps happening. I probably wouldn't have bought the wheel if you hadn't needled me. Well, I'm glad I did. I just hope you're as right about Bea and this stunt."

"I take it you're agreeing with me," he said, already wheeling the pickup into a U-turn.

"Not on everything," Leah reminded him. "I decided that I can stand a few more gray hairs and suffer a minor nervous collapse to allow Bea her moment of glory, hopefully. Don't expect agreement too often or too easily, Jonathon. I'm not the docile, 'yes' girl I once was."

"I wouldn't have you any other way," he said. "Except, I'd prefer a lifetime, not just a week more."

His proposal went unanswered, slipping by without a comment from her. She was as conscious as he was of the date, the pressure of the end closing in. And, more than ever, she was aware how her life, as well as her heart, could be taken over by him. It would take only one word. Yes.

Her resolve to say no was not as firm, as unshakable, as it had been. She knew her ambivalence was growing, and Jonathon sensed it. Lately, there were too many times when Leah felt so closely bound to him, heart and body, mind and soul, that she could not bear the thought of separation, of leaving.

Bound. She mentally chanted that ominous syllable. *Bound to another person's grand design, not hers. Bound to being just a wife and mother without a name, an identity as Leah.* She had been Mrs. for a long time and she would be Mom forever.

And she was being bound, pleasantly and steadily, into Fairharbor. The tight-woven fabric of this community was incorporating her into the warp and woof of daily life. She was meeting people, liking them and forming friendships. Soon she could find herself tied down, limited to a small town's boundaries. *Bound.*

"I think I should have sent her to Mexico," groaned Leah as they pulled up at the wharf. "She could have only gotten the trots, at the worst. No, scratch that! I have more faith in Mother Nature and Beatrice Rose than I would if she was with Michael and his 'Princess.' Bea would be diving off cliffs in Acapulco or dating a Mexican playboy."

"You won't be sorry," he said. "Wait until you see her face when she rows in."

"God, don't let me be sorry," Leah whispered prayerfully. She neglected to mention she was praying for herself, loving Jonathon and knowing she was leaving him, as well as for Bea Rose's triumph.

When Bea appeared by the rocks at the far end of the harbor, Leah was alone on the wharf. Jonathon had left for five minutes to get them cold drinks to battle the afternoon sun's heat. In her anxiety, Leah tripped over a coil of hawser and skinned her knee. She didn't feel the sting and didn't mind shouting herself hoarse, jumping up and down yodeling encouragements as Bea handed in.

Leah tied up the *Jolly Rosie* and knelt down to offer her hand to help Bea out. "You made it!" she exulted. "Stand up and take your bow."

Bea promptly flopped on her back, full length, in the skiff and gulped air noisily through her mouth. Her nose was burned to a bright red and she held out her palms, showing Leah a collection of wicked-looking blisters. But her mouth was drawn up in a triumphant smile and her eyes were brighter than the flashing sun on the water.

"Bury me . . . at sea," she gasped. "Set the *Rosie* afire and . . . give us a Viking funeral."

"Where did you learn about that?" Leah knew the answer as soon as she asked. "Well, we should wait for Jonathon to do the honors, then. Besides, if you can joke, you'll probably live to brag about this."

"Where's Jonathon?" Bea asked peevishly, struggling to sit back up without using her tender hands. "I'll never forgive him if he went looking for me again. I told him I could do it!"

Leah slipped into the skiff to give her some help. Her quick explanation that Jonathon had only gone to buy the victory "champagne" mollified Bea, red-eyed from salt spray and starting to shake from muscle fatigue. She put her arms around Bea, realizing her daughter was too big to lift and carry and still too little to let go of.

The flames of the two white candles flickered in unseen drafts and their glow shrank briefly, threatening to go out, before they came back to a full, golden light. There were flowers in Leah's silver bowl, a bright bouquet Jonathon had picked from his garden and the wilder varieties growing on the cliffs. Her contribution to this romantic evening had been the delicious, overpriced wine they were sipping.

"To us." His toast and the motion of their arms clinking the crystal rims together was responsible for the candlelight's dance.

"To us," Leah repeated.

She had been apprehensive about tonight, but everything was proceeding like one of Bea Rose's fantastic scenarios. They were slightly drunk, not with wine, but with each other, touching without needing an excuse, giving quick glances that were really caresses, part of the ritual of these nights alone. The tension was always there, building until Jonathon or Leah decided the game had gone far enough.

The end was very near tonight. She craved him, as though his body and the things he did with it were a drug. Soon, they would be unable to stop one kiss from becoming ten, a hundred kisses, long and yearning kisses. And then, he would fill her up with love until the hunger was satisfied, the craving muted. She would feel whole and good. So would he.

Until the next time. Leah put her wineglass down, unable to swallow the sip she'd taken. There was no next time and it made all the difference this evening. The day after tomorrow marked the end of her summer job and Fairharbor. She did not want to believe tonight meant the end of love, too, but Jonathon would have something to say about what happened to them.

He drained his glass and set it aside. "I want to talk, not fight."

"Not now."

"When? The guest room is full of empty cartons and those boxes you packed already. You're here with me but you're half gone, too."

"We've talked, Jonathon, and we've fought," she said, keeping her voice pitched low. "And we've loved. I've explained everything I can as honestly as I know how."

"You can't find what you're looking for in a small town or in marrying me," he said. "That's the gist of it."

"I don't know. I'm not sure," Leah whispered, her green eyes filling with tears. Crying would not help, though. She had to make him understand how difficult but necessary her decision was. He did not want to understand, so it was easier for him to think she was cold and callous.

"Then give it more time," rasped Jonathon. "Give me more than three months. Stay! A little longer, at least."

"And do what?" She touched his arm in appeal, withdrawing it when she saw the shadow of pain cross his features. "I'm not going to busy myself coaching soccer, being a volunteer fireman, or doing any of the things that satisfy you. You found yourself, Jonathon...a long time ago."

"Yes," he agreed, "but my life has been infinitely better with you in it. I want to share my life with you."

"But you'll still have a good life and one that you alone chose. I'm still testing my wings, choosing where I want to fly and how high I can go."

"I wouldn't hold you down," he said sadly. "I'm not some anchor. There's a huge ocean two people sail together when they fall in love. The waters aren't always smooth but . . ."

Without warning, Jonathon stood and pulled Leah to her feet. His mouth covered hers hungrily. Leah could counter every other argument but this one. Logic and reason lost importance in his embrace and her heart took over.

Her lips were as eager as his. She traded kiss for kiss, exciting him as much as he did her. But there were trades she must not make, some dim recess of her brain warned, before the response of her body overwhelmed thought.

Happiness in his arms, in Fairharbor or in bed was wonderful, but she would not build her life solely around a man again. She was not content with Leah; even a man as good and decent as Jonathon could not tell her what direction to take, what was best for her.

"I love you," whispered Leah, wishing love was enough, the beginning and end of her search.

When Jonathon edged her toward the couch, she was willing, heated by her passion for him, chilled by the sadness and knowledge it was the last time. He knew, too. There was extra tenderness in his hands when he began to take her clothes off, more tenderness in the play of his fingers across her swollen, straining nipples.

He pushed her down gently and stood over Leah, making love to her with his eyes long before he began to undress. She devoured the sight of him, wanting each second to last a little longer, feeling the urgency in both of them growing.

Jonathon dropped beside the couch, kneeling next to her. His lips brushed her mouth, leaving to inch down to her breast. With the confidence of a lover who has been there before, he licked and teased the aching tips until Leah could not hold still. His mouth traveled on, winding down her length with a light string of kisses, a leisurely, passionate journey to take them to ecstasy together.

When she was crying his name, writhing for the connection of flesh to flesh, Jonathon moved over her. He stayed poised there for a long minute, his hardness resting on the soft skin inside her thigh and yet denied her. Leah reached for him, urging him on in throaty whispers.

"Say it once more," he asked, gazing into her face. "I love you and I need to hear it, to hold the words when I won't have you to hold."

She did, breathlessly, wildly, repeating as his body united with hers, "Yes, I love you . . . yes, yes . . ."

The power of his thrusts, the beauty of the moment they created took over. Jonathon was joined with her body in those deep, slow strokes that stirred and released all the best feelings within her. She could sense the desperation of his love tonight, the need to make it timeless and endless, a hold stronger than any single act of love.

She could not say more than she had, explain or promise more. Leah moved against him, faster and faster, showing him the rapture she felt, the pleasure he gave her. And when she was lifted to the very pinnacle of sensation, her eyes opened, held his to let him see into the depths of her soul. He was forever part of her.

Jonathon stayed motionless for an instant, his face hovering above hers. With a groan more like a sob than anything else, he buried his face between her neck and shoulder. His whole frame shook with not only the force of release but also a tortured sigh, a protest that it had to end.

When she glanced over at the mantle, the candles were winking out. The living room became very dark, very quiet. There were only the funny, intermittent noises an old house makes that used to bother her and Jonathon's quiet, even breathing.

Leah rubbed along his back lightly with splayed fingers. "Upstairs?" she suggested in a whisper. The four-poster bed was wider and slightly less lumpy than the decrepit couch and a better choice for snuggling and sleeping.

"No."

She smiled and kissed the side of his neck, thinking he was as loathe to break the bond of bodies and as replete with a delicious languor as she was. "We'll fall asleep and there's no alarm clock set. I don't think I locked the front door."

He raised himself, taking his weight off her and gently untangling their legs. The moon high outside the window illuminated his shape in a silvery aura, but it was too dark for Leah to see his expression.

"I'm not staying," Jonathon said, rolling away and getting up. "I'm going home, Leah."

"Jonathon?"

He dressed with his back to her, sitting down gingerly on the couch to put his socks and shoes on. There was no contact with Leah's sprawled form, not a single look in her direction, and not a sound from him. Nothing.

She felt uncomfortable, more naked and alone than she could bear in silence. He was shunning her, pretending she wasn't there or gone already. The cruelty of his deliberate avoidance cut her, and the feeling became more anger than discomfort.

"Stop this!" She got to her feet as soon as Jonathon stood up. "For God's sake, Jonathon, is this how you want to end it? Like a cheap one-night stand? I'm hurting, too. We both knew, going into this relationship, our commitment was just to love each other." Her voice wavered. "And I do love you."

"That will be cold comfort when you're in Boston and I'm here dreaming of what might have been."

"I didn't say I'd forget you, stop loving you, did I? You're shutting the door on any future for us. We won't be a world away from each other; we could still see..."

"We can *date*," he said with a mocking tone. "Oh, I know, Leah. We shouldn't have hard feelings. But you see, I do. You love me, but in six months, a year, I believe your fear and distrust of love will be back full force and you won't be back."

"*My* fear? *My* distrust?" The bittersweet evening she had envisioned had become bitter, a sour taste in her mouth. Her body was burning again but not in passion. "I don't see this as my problem, Jonathon. You're the fearful one! I can see it now. I rediscovered that I'm capable of love this summer and you imagine I'll be back there looking for another man…the best man I can find."

She'd had glimpses of his temper and iron will, but until tonight these were only fleeting, short-lived views. As soon as the words were out of her mouth, Leah realized she had unleashed a rare, terrible force in the room. There was almost an electric quality to the air as the storm broke.

The table lamp flicked on and lit Jonathon's scowl. His fury was unmistakable in his rigid posture and the two short steps he took toward her. Leah would have felt safer facing a hurricane, but she would not back down or retract a word.

"No, dammit, I didn't picture you with another man," Jonathon said in an icy voice. "But the idea has obviously occurred to you. I suppose so! I'm the first man you allowed into your life since the divorce, so you have no basis for comparison. Find him and be happy with him, if you can."

She wanted to lash back, to hurt him for his arrogance and stubbornness. "I might," Leah said. "I might do just that while you're here, hiding from the bigger, uglier world, safe from high risks and secure in this little pond."

Snatching the cotton cover from a chair, she wrapped herself in it. Jonathon's face went white and he looked stricken. The pain that filled his eyes was raw, undisguised.

"You think…you think I'm here because I ran away?"

"Oh, my God," gasped Leah, seeing his agony and feeling her own. Her heart constricted as if a vise was tightening around it.

No, she didn't think he was a runaway from success. No more than she dreamed of finding another man to take his place. But, finally, Leah understood that they would part hating each other rather than admit defeat and give in to the sorrow of separation. There was no anguish in her memories of fights with Michael; they'd fought with the careful manners of complete indifference.

She tried to speak and failed. Jonathon reached for her in a helpless gesture, his lips moving silently.

"Forgive me." Leah wept, burying her face into the dusty chair cover. "Oh, I'm sorry..."

"So am I," Jonathon said. He put his arms around her tentatively and withdrew them as quickly. "I love you. I'm sure I always will, Leah. When you can trust me...or trust yourself completely, we'll know how deep love can run for us."

Sobs choked her but she couldn't expect to go to him for comfort.

"If it's for the rest of our lives," he said, "I'll be here for you."

He was gone when she looked up. The front door was left ajar, and she stood there, huddled in the covering and shivering. It didn't serve any purpose, but Leah whispered, "I love you" into the blackness before she went upstairs.

Ten

Sharing a night and knowing it was their last was as bad as Leah supposed it could get. But it was worse when she heard the truck, his step on the porch, the firm knock at the door. He wasn't going to be smiling, ready to kiss her or tease Bea. The loss of any hope of reliving all the moments of laughter and love was far worse.

"It's not locked," she called, reluctant to answer the second knock. He wouldn't give up and go away, not where it concerned her.

She continued wrapping the final batch of her nested bowls in newspapers and tucking them into a wooden crate.

"I'm here to say goodbye to Bea." Jonathon stood at the open door, very still and solemn. "I'll take Tipsy Jane and her many-toed kitten tonight, too. You weren't expecting me to see you off tomorrow morning, were you?"

Leah shook her head, not wanting to hear her voice quaver or squeak. She motioned to invite him in. Instead of stepping forward, he first bent and picked up something hidden from her view on the porch.

Once Leah saw the *Jericho* in his arms, she couldn't have spoken if she wanted to. Jonathon went past her to place the ship on the end table, looking around for Bea.

She cleared her throat, but it had no effect. "Bea Rose's upstairs packing. I'll call her."

"In a minute," Jonathon said. He fixed a stern expression on his face. "The *Jericho*'s yours. Every time you look at her, you'll think of me, Fairharbor and this summer."

And what we've meant to each other. Not everything has to be spoken, he'd told her.

"Yes, of course," Leah replied hoarsely. "I would think about you, anyway. Thank you, Jonathon. I know what she represents, how important this clipper is to you."

"So are you," he said softly. "And you always will be."

For a brief moment, the hard set of his features threatened to change from impassive and commanding to sad. Leah raised her hand to her mouth and felt the quiver of her lips, the danger of tears coming closer. He recovered, knitting his brows together and a stiff determination returning.

"If I ever catch wind that you sold her, I'll..."

"You'll what?" Leah attempted a smile at his show of fierceness. She went nearer to him, intending to kid him and stroke the frown from his forehead, but when she got close enough, she stopped short. There was not going to be more joking and touching. There couldn't be.

"I don't put my feelings on display often and my family history isn't for sale," he growled. "You take this gift and treat her the way I would or I'll swoop to Boston like a typhoon and take the *Jericho* back!"

"Okay," promised Leah. "You needn't worry. I'll always treasure this ship. I know she's part of you."

"Then you'll remember you could have had all of me," he said evenly and quickly turned to call upstairs to Bea.

The truth was painful. Leah was staggered by how much it hurt. When Bea came racing down to hug Jonathon, sniveling loudly, Leah stumbled into the kitchen to regain her composure. The end of a summer romance should not be more painful than the breakup of a thirteen-year marriage and in some ways it was.

She spilled coffee grounds all over the counter and floor. "Damn you!" Her curse was directed at her clumsiness but also at Jonathon. Goodbye would be so much easier if he didn't insist on dragging it out, making the break less than clean and complete. Even his gift was calculated to wound her as much as she had longed and schemed for it.

It has to be. Leah bent her head, blocking out their voices in the next room. A scalding tear escaped before she gathered her strength and held the others back. Clutching at her final decision and wrapping the old protective shell around herself, she knew she would manage.

When she rejoined Bea and Jonathon, her control was restored. Blunting her feelings was a strong defense and a technique she hadn't used—or needed to use—for most of this summer, but it still worked.

"My dad made arrangements for someone to tow *Jolly Rosie* to his slip," Bea was saying. "He and Karen brought me a ton of presents back. I'm dying to know what they are...."

Leah curled at the end of the sofa, removed from them. Bea's weepiness and long face were gone already, another reassurance to her. Her daughter's tears had dried quickly, and she was looking forward to what came next, not what had happened. It took longer to heal, Leah thought, the older you got, but in time it was still possible to bounce back, wiser and surer.

"What about your potting wheel?" Jonathon persisted in trying to bring her into the conversation.

"I'm taking it. It's all set." She resisted, wishing him gone, wishing the night over, and hating herself for acting so cold and detached.

"You write to me, sport, and I'll answer," he said to Bea, holding her close and releasing her immediately. "Go fetch my mousers, will you? There's an able child."

Leah stood up when he did. It seemed appropriate that she felt stiff and dazed, just as she had the night he'd walked into their lives three months ago.

"Sit down," he said harshly. "I know my way out. A handshake would be an insult and a kiss, a lie."

Leah moistened her lips. "Don't . . . don't hate me, Jonathon, please."

"You fool!" Jonathon whispered. He started to say something else and thought better of it, shaking his head and turning away.

There were equally cruel words she might have flung at him. Dreamer, for one. He was an overly romantic, idealistic dreamer. And he was a relic, the kind of man who was in touch with a reality that had faded years ago, out of touch with an urban, contemporary viewpoint.

Leah refused to respond. She kept her face averted and heard his farewell to Bea, the cats' call, and the door closed. Wailing about Jonathon and the cats, her daughter thundered up the stairs to the sanctuary of her bedroom, but Leah could scarcely hear Bea's commotion.

The click of the lock, metallic and very final, seemed as loud as a rifle shot to her.

They were leaving with much more than they had arrived with. Leah took another box from a mute Beatrice and shoved it into place with her knee. She debated whether the drive back to Boston with a sulking, silent Bea would be worse than having to listen to another couple of hours of grousing.

"All right," Leah said on Bea's next trip from the house. "Get it off your chest! Say what's on your mind and let's have it out in the open. You'll feel better."

"No, I won't," grumbled Beatrice, handing over her dress, a bag of seashells, and hugging Barnaby's farewell gift. She refused to hand over the stuffed animal, a white cat, for stowing away.

Leah was having enough difficulty with her own unresolved emotions. She rolled her eyes skyward, appealing to heaven for strength. It was far too early in the morning after too little sleep for a temper tantrum or scene.

"Honey," she said, digging deep for patience and understanding, "you'll be back. We got lots of invitations to come and visit. Think about everything you were looking forward to, instead. Seeing Dad and Karen, Beanie and your friends, telling about the summer, showing them the *Jolly Rosie*..."

She couldn't completely convince herself of how great their return would be. Still, Bea's dubious look and quirked eyebrow were annoying. The longer Leah went on about the total impracticality of staying and complete inevitability of today, the more upset she felt.

"And my job, your school. I can't support us here and Kildear School is not the academy." She searched her daughter's face for a sign of understanding.

"Why won't you marry Jonathon?" Bea asked bluntly. "He'd like us to stay. He wants to marry you, even if he hasn't said it. I can just tell."

Leah thought about resorting to a lie. Or, by rights, she could argue Bea Rose had no business asking questions and offering opinions on adult matters—particularly personal ones. But Bea was told lies by Michael, excusing his behavior or promises he didn't keep. And she herself had told white lies, fibbing to excuse him before their split and to avoid seeing Bea hurt since.

No more lies. Leah rubbed her nose and groped for the simplest explanation. It would be criminal to undo all the good and the closeness wrought by this summer by saying too little or too much.

"Jonathon did ask me," Leah said huskily. "He cares for us both and . . . yes, he knows we care for him."

"Love him," corrected Bea, hanging her head. "Not like Daddy, but I love Jonathon."

"Good!" said Leah and she meant it. "I'm glad to hear you can love lots and lots of people."

Bea had to interrupt to enumerate everyone she was "wild" about in Fairharbor, courageously tacking Barnaby Templeton's name on the end of her list.

Leah hugged her hard. "That's great, honey. But what I was going to tell you—about Jonathon and me—is that marriage is still a very special, important love, a giant step. No one wants to make a mistake, not the kind that involves our lives."

"You said no, in other words."

"I said I wasn't sure," amended Leah, "and I'm not."

"I thought you knew everything," grumbled Bea. "You always sounded like you did."

"Well, we both learned some vital things this summer, then," chuckled Leah. "I'm not infallible and you can row."

"I learned more than that," Bea said, raising her chin to take a long, last look at Chandler House and the vista of town and harbor. "I don't seem to be able to put it into words, Mom."

"Don't worry about it." Leah wrestled the station wagon's door open and got in. "We can talk about it on the drive, or you can wait until you can put your finger on it yourself."

"It's puberty," moaned Beatrice, mashing the cat to her chest.

They started for the highway with Beatrice in full cry about the horrors of maturing. Leah was thankful for the distraction. She had Boston before her and a fair breeze blowing through the windows. There was only a momentary twinge whenever she had to check the rearview mirror and Fairharbor was there, shrinking from a town to a postcard scene and finally disappearing like a dream she was suddenly awakened from.

At first, Katherine Chandler was speechless, no mean accomplishment. She lit a cigarette from the end of the one she'd finished smoking, stubbing out the butt in a huge cut-glass ashtray. She exhaled through her nose, dragon-fashion, and stood up.

"My God, just look at you, Lee!" She came around her walnut slab of a desk to embrace Leah. "I had the sense it was quite a summer but . . ."

"That bad, eh?" said Leah, obediently pecking back at both sides of Kate's face. "The ten pounds are the result of cooking every night. I was there most of the time, so I couldn't plead I was rushed and pass the can opener, please. The hair... well, I let it grow out and do its own thing.''

"Oh, no, you're marvelous," Kate clarified. She fluffed out one side of Leah's long, untrimmed tresses. "Younger, freer, less kempt but less uptight. Wear a wild print and gigantic hoop earrings for our grand opening and play this look up.''

She went to the oatmeal leather couch and patted the spot next to her. Leah understood from the gesture that she was in Kate's good graces, her fair-haired girl. It wasn't always easy to read Kate; she rarely bothered to finish a sentence, expecting people to intuit what she meant.

"I brought the last purchases with me," began Leah. "I poked around the gallery on my way in and I see you've arranged everything I sent already. I would like to have some say about the display. I had a few ideas of my own.''

"Later," Kate said. "We have a week before the official debut. I wanted to talk about what I've decided for you in the future.''

I'll handle the gallery, thought Leah with a twinge of excitement. If she looked like a gypsy to Kate, so be it. Her crystal ball reading was coming true. Leah was so busy juggling figures in her head, deciding which bills to pay off and whether the car would last another year that she missed part of Kate's lavish praise for her summer's work.

"... to a great start. But, of course, the trick will be to keep it going... always bringing in the fresh, unexpected items.''

Leah nodded, unable to keep her mind from wandering. She was fascinated with the color and cut of Kate's hair; it was mauve, hung straight and was chopped off geometrically just above the collar of her amethyst linen suit. Grande dames used to have white hair, tinged with blue or yellow, and didn't have businesses, but charities, as hobbies.

"We lease a car for you. My tax man tells me that everything but drawing breath can be a write-off." Kate blew out a blue cloud of smoke that reminded Leah of the low-lying morning mists over the ocean. "Give some thought to scouring the interior. Every coast town will be Fairharbor, to some extent. Hinterlands, not headlands, next."

"When?" Leah asked dully, trying to catch up. "Next summer?"

"Oh, my dear, before Christmas," Kate said, creasing her forehead. "You bought quite a bit but not . . ."

"I'll be the buyer. The scout." The thrust of the conversation sunk in. Alarm bells started to ring in Leah's ears. No, her plans didn't include traveling the breadth and width of the Bay State year around. She had a child who needed her. Her tentative decision to rent some cheap studio space and keep on potting would be down the drain.

Leah interrupted Kate's monologue on a man near Mount Greylock who was rumored to make these "enchanting" figurines of elves and trolls and mountain gnomes.

"But . . . but before I left, we were discussing my managing the gallery. Bea's in school, not in her own apartment—yet. Michael only sees her every other weekend, if then. I could make arrangements for her, but I don't . . ."

"I sold my interest in Smart," said Kate, referring to the boutique turning out the exquisitely tailored and rather shapeless clothes she wore. "I was bored with it. Organizing and getting Sou'Wester Gallery together was a shot in the arm . . . pure energy. God, if I were younger, I'd prowl the countryside myself."

"I don't know," Leah said, confused. "I have to think about it."

"The salary is okay, isn't it?" Kate frowned. "I did check with my friends on what would be attractive and fair."

"It's not the money," Leah said quickly. "Fairharbor was a tryout for a permanent part. I thought . . . a sort of partnership with you. You'd be busy at Smart and I'd have a steady, full-time job."

"You still can." Kate reached over and patted her hand. "Think it over and let me know. Now I must hear how you survived the Fairharbor experience! Survived? You seem to have thrived, and I was simply tortured by needless guilt after you went."

"I don't have any regrets," Leah said, choosing her words very carefully. "And Bea's summer was, all in all, a good one. She really matured, I think, and enjoyed herself."

Kate looked shocked, as if she'd misjudged Leah's character as well as her sense of taste. "*Really?* Oh, the endurance it took me to spend vacations and holidays with Grandmother Chandler in that wretched house! The town's incredible sameness, the tedium and ennui . . . well, well, you know, having been cooped up there."

"I don't know," Leah replied evenly. "I have some of the most wonderful memories of my life because of the past three months. I met all these new people . . . dealt with characters . . . Bored? No, not once. I hit a few real low points, too, but it was . . ." She discarded the usual superlatives that meant nothing and settled for one that counted. "It was good. I was busy and happy."

There was open disbelief on Kate's face. She went to her desk for another cigarette and said rather sharply, "In that case, I ought to consider selling you the house. I only kept the old mausoleum this long because I never think of it—not if I can help it. The place has a historic and sentimental value for my family, I suppose, but if you were eager to bury yourself and your career options, you couldn't do better than Fairharbor."

Leah was rankled to hear Kate talk about career options. It was doubly aggravating after being denied the very route Leah had felt sure was open for her. The elegant Mrs. Chandler could pick and choose, based on her family's position and wealth.

"Maybe I couldn't do better," Leah agreed, gratified to put Kate off balance for a minute. "I found out how many options I have this summer. There are many more than I thought I had in May. I've taken up ceramics again, for example."

A perfect cigarette ring hung in the air, expanded and then disintegrated. Kate seemed annoyed and made a show of opening her appointment book.

"Bring me a piece or two to look at, why don't you? We could do nice publicity with you as artist and buyer, I'm certain. Seriously, are you interested in the house? As a country retreat . . ."

"I don't think so. I've always seen myself as a city mouse." Leah didn't plan to say more, wanting to slip off to examine this new situation and balance pluses and minuses. She admired Kate but wasn't willing to tell her the whole story. Inexplicably, she heard herself talking, unwilling to let matters rest.

"I had my chance to resettle there and I refused." Leah slung her purse over her shoulder and waded through the soft brown carpeting to the door. "Spending the summer was worthwhile. I felt that spending my life in Fairharbor was too overwhelming a prospect, too drastic a move."

"Drastic? Fairharbor?" Kate laughed. "Oh, Lee, you are being droll. I see."

"Not at all," Leah muttered. "You don't see."

Kate fiddled with her lighter and her eyes assumed a hard glint. "Aha!" she exclaimed with sudden insight. "Who was he? A newcomer or from the old stock? Let me think about it; I recall most of the ancient families when I force myself to."

"Wardwell," Leah said, silently cursing herself for a blabbermouth. It wasn't Kate's business and it was over. How stupid to stir up the hurt and her muddied emotions just by saying his name!

Kate Chandler narrowed her eyes and made a humming sound of agreement. "Yes, Joseph Wardwell... I wasn't allowed to play with those children. Well, they lived...and their father was a bootlegger." She shook her head. "No, you couldn't be speaking of Joseph. Or are you? He's my age... But his wife did die, I heard. Horrors, have I made a faux pas?"

"His son," Leah whispered and realized her throat was getting tight. She would probably disgrace herself and cry if she said Jonathon's name aloud. "I've got to run, Kate. I'll call you or meet you at the gallery later this afternoon."

"The son. The son," Kate muttered and tapped her nails on the desk. "Is he in lobsters, too?"

Leah didn't bother to answer. It didn't matter what Jonathon was "in"; Kate Chandler would think of him as a rube, a coastal bumpkin. Another minute or two and she would have rattled off a list of all the very eligible, fine men she'd introduced Leah to, invited to dinner parties just to meet her.

What was Jonathon *in*? He was in her heart, in her blood. She could not get him out of her mind. Leah went back to the apartment to review what had happened with Kate and found she was staring at the *Jericho* instead. The ship was a link with him, dominating the tiny living room and constantly drawing her eye.

His magnificent gift was not without a price, bringing with it a flood of haunting memories. Her hard work and careful planning to succeed had a price she was not willing to pay. She, too, had built a ship that would never sail because she depended on Kate to back her and believe in her.

Nothing's working, Leah thought in disgust. *I better start from scratch.* She kicked off her shoes and sat at the desk, contemplating the clipper and her prospects.

She was wrong. It took four hours and a missed appointment with Kate at the gallery but her brain was working, her nerve starting to come back. She made coffee and drank from one of her cat mugs, toasting the *Jericho* and Jonathon, in absentia. The answer was in front of her all the time.

"Hi, Mom. What's happening?" Bea Rose grinned and dropped her books. "You're home early, aren't you?"

"Sit down," ordered Leah. "What's happening depends on us, kiddo."

Eleven

———

There was a large plank, sea washed and sun bleached, diagonally displayed. A rusty rivet at one end was matched by a rusty orange velvet drape, a few scattered oak leaves tucked in the folds and apparently carelessly strewn around the rest of the gallery's show window. Nothing about the arrangement was careless, however. Leah had watched Kate's favorite decorator spend most of the afternoon fussing endlessly over the fall and swirl of the cloth, the exact number of leaves, the positioning of each item in the showcase.

Bea squeezed Leah's fingers and flashed her a toothy grin. "You made the big time! Twice! My cat mug and the dopey kid alphabet plate... Are the bucks gonna come pouring in?"

"At the prices Kate's charging, yes." Leah laughed. "I wouldn't have the nerve to charge ten dollars for a cup."

She gave her own work a final glance before they went in the gallery. The simple brown-and-gray plate, incised with letters and numbers, looked right at home next to Arna Templeton's willow basket. She had a right to be proud and a right to be nervous tonight.

The opening was scheduled for seven o'clock. Not many people would show up before ten, a more fashionable hour. Kate wasn't even there yet. Leah walked around, noting that none of her suggestions had been used.

"Ohh, Mom..." Bea's little squeak of surprise came across the room. "You're not selling..."

"No," Leah said loudly, making the mobile of bright mittens and socks sway. "I'm not selling the *Jericho*. I'm letting Kate display it, that's all."

She crossed the tiles, her heels tapping on the floor, and stood with Bea Rose to look at the clipper. Kate had picked the right spot, lighting it against the stark white walls so that the intricate rigging cast shadows and the dark silhouette of the ship was impressively large.

"Jonathon said—" Bea gave Leah a sidelong glance "—the *Jericho* was just for you. I don't think he'd like this."

"I'm sure he wouldn't," Leah replied calmly. "However, the ship's mine. The skiff is yours. If you decide to plant marigolds in it or upholster it and use it as a bed, that would be your choice. I'm not selling it, but I think it's worth seeing."

"But you promised," objected Bea with genuine indignation.

Leah took advantage of Kate's entrance with several people in her wake to distract her daughter. "Go help them set up the buffet and bar," she suggested. "You can sample the food, not the champagne. And let me know when your father and Karen arrive, if I don't see them first. I have to talk to Michael.''

She stood a while longer at the *Jericho* before making a complete circuit of the gallery. A few prompt patrons and browsers had arrived and Leah trailed them, unabashedly listening to their comments. Everything was ''adorable'' or ''quaint'' when it wasn't ''stunning.''

''This piece would be striking mounted in a block of marble on your desk,'' a woman said and received an appreciative laugh for her pun. She was holding a hand-forged weather vane, fashioned into a large cloud with a lightning bolt emerging. ''I always hated that modern whatzit you have.''

''It's a weather vane,'' Leah muttered under her breath, ''not sculpture. Her hypocritical speech to Bea about using the skiff as a planter made her smile; she knew Bea would never do anything to spoil the boat.

A short time ago, Leah would have agreed with the overheard opinions and lavishly praised the Chandler touches in displaying the handicrafts. Tonight she was quiet, listening for the small disturbed note within herself. The gallery was too beautiful for words, more impressive than the items it was featuring.

It shouldn't matter, perhaps, that Arna's baskets were cunningly filled with native weeds, sprayed in high-fashion colors. The baskets were going to sell well and be filled with silver Christmas ornaments to decorate someone's foyer. It did matter, though. The tiny sound inside her said it was false and phony, that baskets made for balls of yarn, magazines and firewood were not merely window dressing.

Familiar faces were appearing. Leah shook hands and chatted with the wives of prominent men, particularly lawyers. She'd served on boards and committees with some of these women and was introduced to many of Kate's friends, their names often recognizable from the society pages. The room was beginning to look and smell like money, the sure sign of success. Undoubtedly, the gallery would be as chic as the dress shop had been.

"There you are," Kate blared at Leah, sweeping up in a wrinkly, rusty silk outfit. She matched her autumn color scheme to a T and jangled with gold every time she took a step. "You must meet that gentleman over by the bar. He's absolutely enthralled by the model ship... beg, borrow or steal it, I think... He'll offer you the world..."

"I don't want the world," Leah said dryly.

Kate assumed a distinctly maternal expression and put one arm gently around Leah's shoulders. "Listen, my dear, I think you're wonderfully brave, striking out on your own at your age. But don't be foolish! Harvey has business contacts you might be able to use. I'll certainly sell lots of your sweet plates and mugs but not enough to keep you housed, fed, clothed..."

"I know, I know," Leah assured her. "I'll only be potting part-time, anyway. I've lined up a regular job, too. Until I have plenty of wares and plenty of outlets, gift shops and what not, I need a steady income. I'll be fine."

"You'll be poor," Kate said sadly. "My friend, the starving artist. Really, Leah! You have a child to think of."

"Bea likes the idea. We discussed it completely, and she understands the financial problems. I've saved a little; we'll skimp a little."

"Michael will never agree to putting her into public school," said Kate in hushed tones as if they were discussing something dirty.

"He'll agree or foot the whole tuition," Leah snapped back. "I went to public school. It didn't ruin my life. Bea wasn't the one who insisted on the academy; Michael was."

"I hope you know what you're doing." Kate's tone indicated she didn't hold much hope. "Well, Harvey is waiting. I'll show him your work and play you up as an eccentric artist. Maybe he owns a chain of department stores I don't know about."

"Thanks," Leah said, giving Kate a hug before she fled.

She went and stationed herself near the *Jericho*, surveying the crowded room for Bea, for Michael and Karen, for anyone from Fairharbor.

Leah snagged Bea by a bony elbow as her daughter made it to the buffet table for her final foray.

"It's half an hour before closing and I want to boogie," she said softly. "Let's go. I don't have to stay; I don't work here anymore."

A cocktail hot dog protruded from the corner of Bea's mouth like a cigar butt. "The food's great and the wine's not bad. Grab a plate."

"*Wine?* Who gave you wine? I'll kill them." Leah prepared to assault the barman, appropriately dressed in a bright yellow slicker, sou'wester hat and white sea boots. Perspiration, not salt spray, glistened on the man's face.

"Daddy did. Just a swallow, not a glass, for pete's sake," mumbled Bea. She swung her arm across the mobbed gallery. "He and Karen just got here, and they already bought a ton of stuff. A cradle, sweaters, one of your cat mugs, too. They're going to do an authentic nursery for the baby..."

"Fast workers," Leah said, spotting Michael. "Let's pray for an authentic baby, then." She tugged on her child to accompany her.

"I want more guacamole," whined Beatrice.

"I'll make beans and franks when we get home. It's ever so authentic for Boston."

It was amazing she had missed Michael. He was, without a doubt, the tallest, handsomest and loudest man left in the place. Naturally, he was holding court, talking and waving around one of the five dozen knit caps. Karen was plastered to his side, looking stunning and laden with goods.

"Lee!" Michael flipped on the thousand-watt smile and switched it off just as quickly. "How nice this is. Karen, Lee's here. You can tell her how great the show turned out."

Karen dimpled. "Your show is great, Leah. We spent over two hundred dollars in ten minutes. I'll bet Bea Rose told you the big news . . . well, actually, it's small news."

"Thanks. Congratulations. Your tan's fabulous," Leah reeled off. "Michael, I've been trying to get a hold of you all week. Can I have five minutes now? I have some news of my own."

"Sure." He nodded and added the hat to Karen's pile. "Only five minutes? Your news can't be all that big, either."

"I'll talk fast," Leah said and gestured toward the *Jericho*, hoping for a little privacy.

She maneuvered her back to the white wall, forcing Michael to focus his attention on her. Otherwise, he would appear to listen and hear nothing, while he scoped out who was here who needed to be impressed or advised. Or worse, who impressed him and required a dignified approach immediately.

"I gave Kate my notice," Leah said, taking a deep breath to make a verbal dash to the finish. "I'm going to get by, financially, but there will be some changes made."

"Not in child support." Michael was already edging sideways, shifting his position to keep the gallery in view. "I've got a new family, not just a new wife."

Gritting her teeth, Leah said, "Unless you'd like to wear some hand-forged andirons home, Michael, you will shut up for once and listen!"

A genuine threat had the desired effect. Michael refused to stand still, but he held steady enough while Leah outlined her plans to follow a new career and the need for Bea to switch schools. When his sarcastic comments on the futility of Leah's turning hippie at her age did no damage, he tried browbeating.

"You're willing to cut our child's options at your expense," he snarled. "Any college worth going to will take her from the academy. But public school?"

"You did all right," Leah said calmly. "I know Bea's going to make it. I have complete faith in her...which is more than I could have said of you. And I'm convinced I'll do very well, thank you."

"I'll see if I can swing the full tuition," Michael muttered. "This is a manifestation of mid-life crisis or second childhood, Leah. You'll come to your senses, I hope."

She laughed, realizing it was the first full laugh she'd enjoyed since they left Fairharbor. "I did, believe it or not."

"I'm sorry," Kate's voice clearly enunciated. "But, you see, the gallery's closing. We will be open at our regular..."

"I'm not here to see your stuff," an irate man objected. "I'm getting what's mine and I'm gone, lady. Now move."

Leah pushed Michael aside, out of her line of vision, and saw Jonathon storm in, an indignant Kate on his heels.

He was thunder rolling across the floor, the bad weather flags flying, but she didn't expect anyone took particular note. They probably noticed an average-sized man in faded jeans and red Windbreaker with a scowl on his face, out of sorts and out of place. She didn't see him that way; her heart pounded savagely, her breath whistled in her lungs and whatever she was saying to Michael was forgotten.

"You!" he hollered, heading for Leah, picking up speed. "I'm glad I made it in time. Lady, you got trouble and a lot to answer for!"

He jostled one man and came closer, oblivious to Michael's repeated inquiries as to who this person was and what he wanted.

"Jonathon," Leah said happily. She took pleasure in saying his name. The sight of him, mad or not, capped the evening. It was Christmas and the Fourth of July suddenly.

"Don't 'Jonathon' me," he yelled, "and give me those big bright eyes, Leah. I'm honked off. I gave you a gift and I don't appreciate seeing it on display without my say-so."

"Right to the point," said Leah. She smiled thinly at Michael. "I really admire that in a man."

Jonathon braked to a stop before he bowled either of them over, but just barely. As far as he was concerned, the need for discussion was ended; he looked at the *Jericho* and back at Leah. The taller, dapper man at his elbow might just as easily have been a nattily attired pillar of salt for all the attention Jonathon gave to him.

Her ex liked people to know who he was.

"Look, fellow, whoever you are...I'm an attorney. We heard Ms. Chandler refuse you admittance. Trespassing and making threats can be a serious..."

Michael went on for a while, hearing only himself, talking to himself and not aware of it. Leah didn't mind. It gave her a chance to look and marvel at the two men who had meant the most to her.

When she examined Michael, she saw not only him but the reasons she had once loved him. He was the epitome of success, glib and attractive, daily dousing himself with confidence and expensive cologne. He had been a junior version when she'd married him and hadn't really changed, only polished and perfected himself. Michael had grown smoother and richer and never grown up. It was no longer a mystery to her why he would have turned to a nineteen-year-old bride, another adoring admirer as Leah once was.

Watching Jonathon, however, gave her clues as to who she had become. He listened politely but disinterestedly to Michael, unimpressed with appearance or bluster. He had worn hand-tailored suits well, too, and had had his hair styled, but now it was trimmed by a local barber. He could have charmed with as much ease as Michael or traded in as much bull, but Jonathon didn't. He wouldn't.

"You give a whale of a speech," Jonathon complimented Michael as he ground to a halt. "If I had a harpoon, I'd let the hot air out of it and throw the minnow of intellect back."

"Who is this guy?" Michael asked, getting no response.

"I want her back," Jonathon said. He stood toe to toe with Leah, giving her the full force of an icy stare.

Michael straightened his tie and made the rumbling in his throat that signaled a speech about to be delivered.

"There's some misunderstanding here. I'm not with this lady. Leah's my ex."

"And I'm not talking to you," Jonathon retorted, without bothering to glance in Michael's direction. "Shove off, Mr. Mackey."

"Now wait just one..." Michael took a half step forward, interposing his shoulder between Leah and Jonathon. He wasn't used to being dismissed or ignored.

Finally, Jonathon did look at him. He moved only his head, not his body, and finished the argument before it began. The two men stared at each other for less than a minute, saying nothing, but there was obviously some strong form of communication that bypassed Leah.

Her ex-husband had no difficulty understanding the gist of the message. "Excuse me," Michael said politely, and he circled behind Leah, not taking his eyes off Jonathon, and walked stiff-legged back across the floor.

"I think you scared him!" Leah exclaimed softly. "That's one for the books."

"Well, it's plain I don't scare *you*. So I've been on the turnpike for two hours with Miranda screeching in my ear and fighting every dingy Boston driver..."

"Where's Miranda?" cried Leah with delight, craning her neck. "I didn't think she'd come, too."

All his menace disappeared and was replaced with exasperation, not anger. Jonathon made a helpless gesture with his hands.

"What is this? A reunion? When Miranda called me and blabbed about this show including the *Jericho*, I was pretty hot, let me tell you. I came to get my clipper back and Miranda came to make sure I didn't do anything nasty."

"It's impossible for you to be nasty," said Leah, "and your aunt knows that as well as I do. I'm not worried or scared."

She raised her hand to his cheek, feeling the slightly rough texture and the warmth that was Jonathon. The dawn of understanding lightened the blue of his eyes.

"What the hell is this about?" he asked hoarsely. "You planned to get me down here, didn't you?"

"It's hard to rout you out. You said so yourself. And there was absolutely no way for me to get to Fairharbor for a while."

"The phones work," he said in a clearer voice. "What do we have to talk about that we didn't cover before you left?"

"I'm not quite sure." She draped her arms around his neck. "Somehow I thought we'd have more to say face-to-face. Oh, Jonathon, is it only two weeks? I've missed you so much, it feels like a year."

"A thousand years," he corrected, putting his hands at her waist. The last shadow of his confusion melted away with a smile. "Tell me this means what I think it does...and tell me fast. I thought you were selling her and I wanted her back."

"Her or me?"

"Lee!" Kate's strident voice was a most unwelcome interruption. "We simply must close."

Ms. Chandler looked unusually harried, uncharacteristically nervous as she approached Leah. It wasn't hard to figure out why as soon as she got closer, Miranda Murching and Bea Rose dogging her steps.

"Purple hair, gold fingernails," Miranda was saying in astonishment. "Katherine, you look a fright! Women our age..."

"I didn't realize you two knew each other," Leah said innocently. She squeezed Miranda as hard as she dared and got a bear hug back.

"Give me the keys to your apartment," Miranda demanded immediately. "I'm sure Katherine would love to give Bea and me a lift there and catch up on the old days. I've got to rest my bunions and tonight's late movie is *Return to Peyton Place*."

"We're closing," Kate said pleadingly to Leah.

Leah pressed her house keys into Miranda's gnarled fingers. "I'll lock up here. I'm not budging a step until Mr. Wardwell and I settle the matter of who owns the *Jericho*. It shouldn't take us long. Bea Rose, you and Miranda share the sofa bed tonight. That way, you can fall asleep during any dull parts."

Kate squared her shoulders and, making a small resigned sound, became her gracious, dignified self. "All right, Miranda, my chauffeur is outside. Promise we won't talk about when we were little girls in Fairharbor?"

"Of course not," Miranda was saying as they left. "I really want to know why you didn't get married and if you had a face-lift."

Bea Rose turned back and grinned in delight, waving at them.

Leah wasted no time locking the gallery door and dimming the lighting. Jonathon studied his own handicraft, not her progress. When she came back and put her arms around him from behind, he seemed actually startled by the contact and he didn't turn to embrace her.

"No kiss?" asked Leah, putting her cheek against his back. "I thought you'd be happier to see me. Especially knowing I wasn't breaking promises. I don't go back on my word."

"You haven't told me why I'm here," Jonathon said.

She laughed to herself. "You haven't given me a chance, not really. Now I haven't ever done this before, so bear with me. Jonathon Jericho Wardwell, I am asking you to marry me."

He spun around and took her head in both his hands, tilting her face slightly up to stare into her eyes. "You better not be... Yes! Yes! My God, yes."

"The third time's the charm," she said very softly. "I fancy that I'm very modern, proposing to a man, and I wasn't sure such a die-hard traditionalist as you would stand for it."

"I can stand a lot with you... or from you," he whispered. His hands held her steady while his mouth came closer and closer to hers. "You should tell me all about this change of heart, but first..."

When the kiss ended, Leah was barely able to tell him her name, and her heart was pounding at an alarming rate. She actually stammered a few times, far more absorbed in his face and the feeling of being held than in rehashing the past two weeks of agonizing.

"I made up my mind about quitting and taking a different job that would allow me to develop as a potter. Alone! *My* decision," emphasized Leah. "And I knew I was right, that I could say I had found out who Leah was and what she wanted. I think you know the rest, Jonathon."

"Maybe I do," he said, rubbing his thumb on her mouth and stroking her eyebrows as if he doubted the reality of her. "You can do whatever you planned without me and you'll be happy, but not as happy as we could be together."

"Yes, I wanted you, too." She hugged him tightly, closing her eyes. The warmth she felt was Jonathon, the scent was laundry detergent and sea breezes, and if she let her imagination take over, they were in Fairharbor in a sunny meadow or walking on the beach.

"You have me. You always did," Jonathon said, pressing his chin onto the top of her head so she couldn't look up.

She heard the emotion in his voice, though, and suspected there were tears rimming the medium-blue eyes. "I took charge of my life, Jonathon, and I realized I wasn't scared. It's exciting. It'll be exciting, no matter what town I'm in. I have big plans and I know you will help and encourage me; that's not dependence."

"That's love," he said. "I will be there for you, always."

She struggled a little and he loosened his embrace. Stretching up, Leah kissed the damp corners of his eyes, his nose and finally his mouth. She wanted to thank him for giving her back the belief in "always" but there was going to be years and years for long discussions, sharing secrets and dreams.

"I'm still not sure about babies," she confided. "I have to be honest. I don't feel too old, mind you, but I got this wild idea about buying Chandler House and turning it into a studio and handicrafts store. Maybe it's too ambitious..."

"We'll talk about it," said Jonathon with a smile that produced a lone dimple. "As for children... well, I think two mature adults can negotiate and compromise. I can be pretty persuasive when I want to be."

He nuzzled her neck and shifted his body next to hers, taking a wide-legged stance to pull her into closer and more intimate contact. Leah began to have a very clear idea of the powers of persuasion.

"Let's go tell Bea and Miranda," Leah suggested, gently nibbling his ear. "If we wait for a commercial, it shouldn't interrupt their steamy movie viewing too much."

Jonathon made no move to leave. He swiveled his head around and kept her in the unbreakable circle of his embrace. "We could wait until the movie is over. I've got some ideas of my own that would be better expressed right here, right now. Noisy, lengthy and very private doings."

"After only two weeks?" Leah made a throaty sound, interested and agreeable.

His mouth swooped down on hers, ending any discussion. The thrust of his tongue matched the roll of his hips until her body answered for her, teasing back, arching forward to meet him. The storm of love she felt for him roared in her ears, making Leah sway with the power of it.

"There's Kate's office..." Leah's voice was a faint whisper lost in the hurricane of the passion they were caught in.

"I want you now," he growled, as stubborn as ever. His fingers caught the hem of the full skirt, sliding it up until he was touching her with equal skill and urgency.

"Here? On greige sculptured plush?" Leah laughed weakly and stopped altogether when his fingers reached their objective.

"It's not as nice as Powhatan Meadow," he whispered, "but it will do, for right now. And making love is an art."

The bold search of her thighs and the continuing massage of his fingers, his cupped hand at the juncture of her legs made speech difficult. Thinking would shortly be an impossibility.

"We're too old for this . . ." she gasped. There was evidence to the contrary in the readiness of her body, the hard flesh he offered her.

"We'll never get too old." He was sliding inside her, finding there was no argument, no resistance, but hot, sweet welcome. "We'll practice this art until we're perfect."

"Oh, Jonathon . . . Jonathon, you're—"

He silenced her with an intensely passionate and convincing kiss. However, Leah had no intention of letting the matter rest. Later, she would tell him. There were a million men richer, smarter, better-looking or more successful but she would still tell him. Jonathon was the best.

Silhouette Desire

**Available
January 1987**

NEVADA
SILVER

The third book in the exciting
Desire Trilogy by Joan Hohl.

The Sharp brothers are back, along with
sister Kit...and Logan McKittrick.

Kit's loved Logan all her life and, with a little
help from the silver glow of a Nevada night,
she must convince the stubborn rancher that
she's a woman who needs a man's love—not
the protection of another brother.

Don't miss *Nevada Silver*—Kit and
Logan's story and the conclusion
of Joan Hohl's acclaimed
Desire Trilogy.

DT-C-1

ATTRACTIVE, SPACE SAVING BOOK RACK

Display your most prized novels on this handsome and sturdy book rack. The hand-rubbed walnut finish will blend into your library decor with quiet elegance, providing a practical organizer for your favorite hard-or soft-covered books.

Only $9.95

Approximately 16" x 8" when assembled

Assembles in seconds!

To order, rush your name, address and zip code, along with a check or money order for $10.70 ($9.95 plus 75¢ postage and handling) (New York residents add appropriate sales tax), payable to *Silhouette Reader Service* to:

In the U.S.

Silhouette Reader Service
Book Rack Offer
901 Fuhrmann Blvd.
P.O. Box 1325
Buffalo, NY 14269-1325

BKR-2

Silhouette Desire

COMING NEXT MONTH

RAGE OF PASSION—Diana Palmer
When Maggie fled from her ex-husband to Texas, she never expected to find an ally in Gabriel, her childhood enemy. Could their feelings flare into love?

MADAM'S ROOM—Jennifer Greene
The joint inheritance of a mansion with an illicit history brought Margaret and Mike together. The house inspired her secret fantasies, but Mike convinced her that his love was sweeter than dreams.

THE MAN AT IVY BRIDGE—Suzanne Forster
Years ago Chloe had seen a mysterious man near her estate, the same week that her step sister disappeared. Could Nathanial be the phantom who'd left his mark on her heart?

PERFECT TIMING—Anna Cavaliere
Olivia had only requested Jonas for an evening, and he played the role of her husband perfectly. But Jonas had other ideas and was determined to make their "marriage" real.

YESTERDAY'S LOVE—Sherryl Woods
The IRS had sent Tate to audit the books of Victoria's antique shop and her complete lack of organization drove him wild. But it soon became clear that opposites do attract!

NEVADA SILVER—Joan Hohl
The third book in Joan Hohl's trilogy for Desire: Kit Aimsley, the half sister of the hero of *California Copper* (Desire #312), and Logan McKittrick— a man she's known all her life—discover the love they share.

AVAILABLE NOW:

TOO HOT TO HANDLE
Elizabeth Lowell

LADY LIBERTY
Naomi Horton

A FAIR BREEZE
Ann Hurley

TO MEET AGAIN
Lass Small

BROOKE'S CHANCE
Robin Elliott

A WINTER WOMAN
Dixie Browning

Coming February
from Special Editions—
The final book in Nora Roberts's sensational
MacGregor Series

For Now, Forever

The MacGregor Series, published in 1985, followed the
lives and loves of the MacGregor children. We were
inundated with fan mail—and one request stood out:
Tell us about Daniel and Anna's romance!

For Now, Forever is that Story...

Anna is a proud, independent woman determined
against all odds to be a surgeon. Daniel is ambitious
and arrogant, a self-made tycoon who wants a woman
to share his home and raise his children. Together they
battle each other and their feelings as they try to make
their own dreams come true.

Look for *Playing the Odds*, *Tempting Fate*, *All the
Possibilities* and *One Man's Art*, all to be reissued in
February in a special Collectors Edition.

Don't miss them wherever paperbacks are sold.